MOTH WANTED

A DARK MOTHMAN MONSTER ROMANCE

MONSTERS IN THE BED.

LOKI RENARD

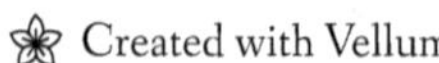 Created with Vellum

1

C *lang.*

That is the sound of a human in captivity.

I've heard it a thousand times before, but it never signified my own capture. How many times have I locked people away? How many times have I closed the door on their wide eyes and left them to suffer the consequences of their actions? I never really gave it too much thought before now. I always assumed I was doing the right thing.

Now I'm starting to wonder if I've ever done the right thing. This time, I am on the wrong side of the door. This time, I am the one who has run afoul of authorities who have declared themselves to have dominion over me whether or not I agree it it. In this scenario, I am no officer of the law. I am a rebellious captive who will be broken to the will of a force greater than me.

I am in trouble.

The shackles around my wrists are metal and familiar. What's less familiar is the chain attached to the D ring attached to the wall, all of it inexorably, and perhaps even inevitably, attached to me.

Was there any other way for this to end?

Here I am, a female cop in her own cuffs. They make a lot of independent cinema about this very predicament. Much like the scenes in those many independent short films, I find myself in a state of vulnerable undress and at the mercy of an inhuman creature. I am naked. Exposed. There is no comfortable position I can assume, nothing that gives me any kind of modesty. I am on the floor, naked with my legs splayed for comfort.

The creature who put me here has not abandoned me to captivity the way I would. He is standing over me, his powerfully strange frame casting a monstrous shadow over me. Red eyes roam my body. My belly seems to be swelling up. Does terror make you retain water?

"You have to let me out." I try begging, though I know it will not work. It never worked on me. Not any of the times people pleaded to be let go.

"There's no out," he drawls. "Not from here. This place was designed to keep *monsters* in. You are only human. You have no chance of escape."

"That's why I'm *asking* you to let me out, asshole."

That was not polite, or diplomatic. I find it very difficult to maintain my temper in a situation like this. I'm not good at appeasing people — or nightmarish chimera beasts, for that matter.

"You always were a bad girl. Never wanted to behave yourself," he purrs intimately. I feel parts of my body tightening with fear and lust. Nothing has been the same since I became this creature's captive. I don't recognize myself, or my desires.

"I'm an NYPD detective!"

"You think that automatically makes you a force for good?"

"Of course not, but I did my best. I got more than one monster off the streets."

He chuckles. "You count me among those monsters, don't you."

I jangle my chains. "Wouldn't you? Hard to consider you a good guy when this is what you do to me after I helped you."

He leans down toward me, and unfurls an appendage unrecognizable to most humans. We do not have these soft, unfurling, agile parts.

"You tried to run away. I can't allow that. I want you, and I intend to keep you. Do you understand that, detective? You belong to me. Every inch of you. Every piece of you. Every breath, every scream, every one of your delicious orgasms. Mine."

He is toying with me, soft, strange tendrils finding the most intimate and wet parts of me. I want to resist him. I tell myself I do, anyway. But I cannot. He is horrendously large, and I am only human. I am not made to resist this kind of power and alacrity of seduction. He has mapped my body and made it his own. He has found every secret spot capable of sending traitorous pleasure to the core of me, and he is hitting each of them in order, leaving me to twist against my cuffs as he seduces and dominates me in equal measure.

I scream in climax and hopelessness entwined, a shriek of release and of despair. It is a sound that excites my captor. He looms over me, the shadow of his great wings falling over me, his hair casting a curtain around our faces. I lose myself in his possessive gaze: eyes that hold no trace of humanity at all and yet still captivate me entirely.

I wish I could blame this all on the monster who now holds me captive, but in the final analysis, it was my actions that brought me to this point, a series of strange events and even odder decisions, all mixed up in a milieu of murder.

~

A *week or so ago...*
It is my thirty-third birthday, and I am standing over a mutilated corpse.

This is not the worst birthday I've had.

"Do you think that's appropriate, detective?"

"What?" I glance up toward the scene guard. She's some poor soul holding a handkerchief to her nose and mouth and refusing to leave the unfortunate corpse to his own devices. These little acts of bravery and quiet displays of strength from beat cops always get me. She could be like her partner, off vomiting in a trash can, but she's made of sterner stuff. She'll go far.

The officer gestures toward my head. Oh. Right. The pink party hat. I pluck it off my head and stuff it into my pocket. I already have a reputation for being a weird, heartless bitch, I don't need to add to that with inappropriate headgear.

There's a good reason for me being pulled away from my small office birthday party. A man has been torn nearly in two.

He is spilling out all over himself, a mess of human. The sheet they tried to cover him with is soaked with the contents of his guts. The smell is horrendous. The sight is worse. But the smell is also... no. The sight. The sight is definitely... hmmm, but then the smell sort of clings to you when you try to walk away, whereas the sight will only play in my trauma nightmares. Still, six of one, half a dozen of the other.

Forensics is going to do their job, take pictures, get amongst the goo. That's not my job. I get to glance at the nightmares, then treat them like a jigsaw puzzle. I wish I could say I've never seen anything like this before, but that wouldn't be true. I've seen this before too many times and all too frequently of late. There is a murderer stalking the city. A killer with a chaotic and disturbing signature.

"Any witnesses? Who found the body?"

"I believe you've got a witness in custody, detective," the officer says. "But I don't think you're going to like what he says."

"What does he say?"

I don't know why I'm asking. I already know the answer. I'm just hoping she doesn't say it.

"He says a moth did it, ma'am."

Fuck.

❧

I leave the scene examination to forensics and return to the 89th precinct. The witness has been installed in an interview room that is doing absolutely nothing for his peace of mind.

He's sitting in the steel chair shaking involuntarily. Some of that might be out of shock and disgust at what he's just seen, but it's also typical behavior for someone undergoing withdrawals. I'm going to bet he was as high as a kite when he saw the moth, just like everybody else who has allegedly seen this monster.

He's about thirty, and is wearing an oversized band t-shirt, tight jeans, and leather boots. He's skinny, and his hair is brown with that stringy quality you get when you decide washing your hair is a capitalist conspiracy. He has the vibe of a young Shaggy who just saw a ghost for sure.

"Chet Smithers?" I check my clipboard as I walk into the room. His basic details have been taken already, as well as a statement that makes absolutely no fucking sense. "I'm Detective Holmes."

"Hey," he says. He has a Californian accent, a chill drawl that persists even though he's terrified. "Dude. That was fucked *up*."

"Yes," I agree. "I'm sorry you had to see that. It was a very disturbing scene."

"It was eating him, man." As he starts to tell me his story, his tremors increase until he is shaking from head to toe. His eyes are rimmed with red, his skin is yellowed and sallow. Fear and a comedown make him look a lot like a zombie, but I'm not going to report an undead creature in interview room two. Because zombies aren't real, and neither are moths who eat people.

"Speaking of eating. What do you want to eat? You look hungry."

He looks sick to his stomach, but he also looks like he needs food.

"Uhhh..."

I go to the vending machines and get the guy a hot chocolate and a protein snack bar. He needs something in him if I'm going to get something like sense out of him.

When I get back and give him the stuff, he looks at it like he doesn't know what it is for a moment or two, then sets about demolishing it. As he does, he tells me a story.

"It was a man. But not like a man, man. He was weird. He was like, twenty feet tall, with red eyes and wings. And his teeth were sharp, and his hands were clawed, and he was just ripping into that poor guy, shaking him, like the way antelopes shake on those nature shows when a pride of lions is eating their insides. You know, the guy was gone, but still moving and..."

This is the sort of eyewitness testimony I am supposed to conduct investigations with. If any of my witnesses were sober, I might get somewhere. But you don't get sober witnesses in Brooklyn after three in the morning. You get the sort of people who see monsters everywhere. They should be looking in the mirror.

"Alright. Do I have all your contact details? You got a cell phone? Twitter account?"

"Uhhh... "

"Write them down," I say, sliding paper over to him with a pencil. I might get some sense out of him tomorrow. I'm not keeping him overnight, and I'm not going to hammer him with questions while he's addled on whatever he's on.

It's time to turn my attention to the victim, identify him, inform next of kin, ask them if there was anybody who wanted to gut him like a fish.

~

"Where's your hat?"

My partner's greeting is drowned out by high-pitched and yet hoarse barking from the emotional support animal who inhabits the top of her desk like a pointy-eared gremlin. Obigor the little Brussels griffon had ginger fur once, but now he is nearly entirely white around his little face. Obigor doesn't see well, doesn't hear basically at all, but he loves Tessie more fiercely than any creature on the planet.

Tessie has worked with me for six months. She holds down the office while I go out and look at things. She does the paperwork, I do the grunt work. She used to go out in the field but got benched after being shot after less than a year on the job by some asshole who didn't want to pay a speeding ticket. She walks with a cane, which she uses to hit people if she catches them feeling sorry for her.

She's very pretty, with caramel skin and the cutest freckles that dot the bridge of her nose, dark eyes, and curling dark hair. She might be the smartest person I've ever met. She can do more from behind a desk in one hour than some people can do in weeks in the field.

"No festive headgear allowed at crime scenes," I tell her. "Why are you still here? You should have been at home in bed hours ago."

"I don't sleep," she says. What she doesn't say is she doesn't sleep because she's always in pain. She refuses to take painkillers besides weed, the scent of which I pretend does not perpetually permeate my office.

"We've got another one," I tell her. "This one looks like a..."

Tessie glances toward our open office door. I share my office with her, which is fine because I'm barely ever here. So really, it's her office.

I've been told to tone down my colorful similes. There's nobody here to hear them, aside from the night shift, but the night shift rarely undergoes the formality of actually appearing at the 89th. They're around somehow without ever being present.

"Another one of them mutilated?" She guesses correctly.

"Yes," I say. Understatement is best.

She pulls out a red file. Everything is stored on computers, of course, but Tessie likes having special case files on paper.

No matter how much they push us to digitize, a lot of us are still addicted to paper. Can't hack a pen.

"Digital pictures are on the computer," she tells me. "Print them out if you want. Wouldn't recommend it. From what I saw, it's a 'cannot be unseen' sort of situation. While you were interviewing the witness, we had some basic stats come through about the victim. Male, somewhere between thirty and fifty. Hard to tell when someone is, er, *open* that way. It's starting to look like a serial killer. If this keeps up, the FBI will be all over it. They love serial killers."

I stare at her and snap my fingers. "That's right! They will be all over this pretty soon. Oh. Good. They can deal with the interviews. And the bodies."

"The tabloids are going to be full of it again. People are getting scared," Tessie sighs.

"People are always scared."

It's not that I'm indifferent, it's that I've seen too much in my time on the force to expect anybody to feel anything other than fear, generally speaking. The world is a much more fucked up place than most people realize. The proper response to waking up each morning is probably five solid minutes of good solid screaming before attacking the day.

"Try and keep it out of Randy Carrot's hands, if you can. This department is still leaking like a fucking sieve," I tell Tessie.

Randy Carrot is not the woman's real name. Her real name is Ramona Carrick. The misnomer is immature, unprofessional, and prime cop humor. One step up from writing her number in the john and noting it is for a good time.

Someone in the force is already having a good time on her payroll. Things that should be kept quiet keep showing up in the tabloid she writes for. Still, that's another problem that isn't strictly mine to deal with, so I won't be dealing with it. That's the Chief's department. Nobody survives this job without learning to delegate and compartmentalize.

"I'm not on speaking terms with Ms Carrick," Tessie says, taking her curly hair down, and then putting it up again, in the way she does when she's agitated.

"Alright, good. I'm going to step outside for a second. Get some fresh air. Try to clear my head."

"Don't forget your lighter," Tessie grins.

"Aw, shuddup." I smile back.

I quit smoking three years ago, and I'm very proud of that fact. Now I only smoke socially, and late at night, and sometimes during the day, and occasionally when I'm alone. I step out the back of the station with one of those blessed cylinders between my ring and index fingers. I need this. I've earned this.

"Detective Holmes!" A raspy voice greets me as I step out the precinct into what should be private property. A camera flash reminds me that it is not.

"Carrot," I sigh.

Randy Carrot is a young woman who seems older. Twenty-five going on fifty-five. She has riotous red curls that fall to her shoulders and emanate out sideways at that point, like an attempted mane. She speaks with a thick New York accent from the outer boroughs. She perpetually sounds like she's smoking a cigarette, though I don't believe she actually smokes.

Her face is pretty, but her green eyes are slightly buggy, big and wide and always staring out at the world with a fascination linked to any given tragedy's potential to make her money. She's shrewd, smart, callous, careful, and let's just say I'm glad she's a journalist and not a criminal, because we'd never catch her if she was.

She gives me a saccharine bright grin, the kind people give you when they wish they could fucking kill you. I do not like Ramona Carrick, but that's not surprising. Nobody does. It's interesting to see that the feeling appears to be mutual.

"You're up late," I note.

"Evil never sleeps, and neither do I. Heard there's another body. The Brooklyn Gutter strikes again."

"The Brooklyn gutter? You referring to plumbing?"

"No. The way he"—she makes a sort of slashing motion with her claw-like hands—"guts them. Flays them."

"What about the Brooklyn Flayer, then?"

"Well, no," she says, turning her eyes skyward to think. "Flay is the wrong word. Plus, people might mistake flay with fillet."

"It's not easy finding a cute way to sell murder stories to a dumb public," I pretend to sympathize.

"It's really not. What can you tell me about the latest victim?"

"He's dead."

She smirks at me. "Stellar detective work. No wonder the killer is still roaming free. Are you even trying to catch him? Or are you just waiting for him to get bored and give up? There are half a dozen families looking for answers, you know."

"Alright, have a good one," I say, turning around and walking back inside. No cigarette for me, I guess. I have work to do, anyway. No need to take a few minutes for myself. Or check my phone. Or think about anything other than the bloody corpses that dance in my thoughts every second of every fucking day.

"Anything come in off the wire, Tessie?"

"Not so far," she says, sitting up. She was asleep on the desk, her head on her hands, her little dog curled up in her lap. She's sitting cross-legged on her chair, giving the little fucker a comfortable place from which to lurch and lunge at passersby. Obigor's a biter, but he only has a few teeth left, so it's not really that bad.

"I'm going to guess none of the store cameras, web cameras, or fucking cell cameras picked up this alleged monster, yet again?"

"No, ma'am. Not so far. Won't know until the morning."

"I'm going to go to the morgue. See if they have anything."

Under normal circumstances, the body wouldn't be processed until tomorrow. However, I happen to know that there is another night owl busy at work in forensics who will have metaphorically leaped upon this body the second she heard about it.

I lona Hefe is the sort of person who likes the morgue because it is quiet. I hear her tools clinking gently as I enter the hallowed space. This place has always felt something like a chapel to me. This is where we make our last attempts to atone to those who have passed, to care for those who were not cared for, and to help bring them justice. Perhaps even peace.

"Sally!"

Ilona always uses my first name. She refuses to stand on formality. I don't like people using my first name. Feels a little too personal. Disrespectful.

"Ilona."

"They're all the same," she says. Ilona has beautiful dark skin and eyes. Her raven hair is always shining beneath the harsh fluorescents and medical lights. If you asked me to describe her, I'd be very tempted to use the word Goth, but it doesn't suit her at all. Beneath her laboratory coat, she is wearing a bright pink sweater and deep fuchsia pants. Her feet are clad in what I strongly suspect are expensive, limited edition sneakers. But bright clothing does nothing for her, not in the context of this inherently dark place. There's a shadow over this woman that all the neon in the world cannot illuminate.

"What are all the same?"

"The patterns," she says, gesturing toward the poor bastard on her table. There seems to be even less of him now. I guess some parts have been taken for testing or similar.

"I've said it before, and I'll say it again. Someone, or something, is feeding on these people. The wounds correspond to rasp marks. They haven't been cut open in the traditional way. They've been sort of chewed through by something with mouthparts."

"So I'm looking for something very large with mouthparts."

She looks at me through her spatter-proof eye protection glasses. Unfortunately for me, they have indeed seen some spatter. Bits of person get in between our shared eyeline. "Like an oversized snail, maybe? Some snails are carnivorous."

"I think we would have noticed a man-eating mollusk on the loose in New York, Ilona."

"It's surprising what you can miss," she says. "Besides. It might not be a man-eating mollusk singular. It could be a small host of them. Perhaps a few hundred. You know, they could be chancing upon the bodies very shortly after post-mortem and destroying the evidence."

"So I am looking for someone who kills people, then uses a specially bred snail horde to destroy the evidence."

"It would be an incredible way to do it. Very smart. Very unexpected."

"Are there snail droppings? Anything to indicate the presence of these creatures? Slug trails?"

"Well," she says. "No."

She seems disappointed that I brought up that inconvenient question. Ilona is good at what she does, but her additional speculation is rarely useful.

"What else is of note? Besides the consumption marks, as yet identified?"

She gives a little shrug. "I'm still waiting for several of the tests to come back. Most of them won't be run until tomorrow at the earliest, and more likely, next week."

This is why the long arm of the law takes so much time to get to anything. Criminals don't have to wait for tests and processes. They can just go out and do crime whenever they feel like it. This person, this awful murderous monster, has the luxury of deciding what his work day looks like. I'm going to be waiting for results for one thing or another until I retire.

I am left with eyewitness reports. I end up sitting in a twenty-four-hour diner going over notes on my phone.

- Red eyes.

- Very tall.

- Wings.

These three descriptors pop out again and again and again. At this point, if I don't take them seriously, I'm ignoring evidence. Ignoring evidence is a bad idea unless you want to be a shitty cop, which I suppose I don't want to be.

"This is some Scooby Doo shit," I murmur to myself.

My eyes are starting to go blurry. I can only sleep when exhausted, and I'm definitely getting there. The sun is starting to rise as I drag my ass into my apartment.

It is cold, messy, and small. None of these things matter because I spend less than eight hours a day here. I live out in the city. This is just where I crash. I could easily live in one of those tiny Japanese apartments where your bed is basically your bath, or whatever. I essentially live in one anyway. The size of this place is under a hundred square feet.

I save room by not having a kitchen. Sure, I have a place where they put counters in and a sink, but I haven't entertained the concept of kitchen any more than that. I put a big, old bookshelf I inherited from my grandmother where the refrigerator would usually go. The cabinets designed for cookware and dinnerware are all full of books. I put up shelves everywhere I could, and all those shelves are likewise full. If I have one vice, it's book collecting. A lot of these tomes come from library sales and flea markets. The rest of them come from the depths of the internet, niche tales from niche authors who engage in niche narratives.

Unfortunately, even though every single spare inch of space has a book jammed into it, there's still not quite enough in the way of storage. There are piles of books here and there on the floor from where I have attempted to order them. I trip over one of them, sending it sprawling over a rug with a nautical compass theme which spreads over much of the floor. It's an old family heirloom, that's what I tell myself. I got it at a flea market, and logic dictates that it was probably someone's family heirloom before it got hocked for drugs or whatever.

My bed is a single mattress on the floor directly underneath the windows. Well, I say floor. I got an old door, raised it up on both sides with some milk crates and I use the underside of it for... you guessed it. More books.

The place smells like old paper, and I love it. When I am here, I am insulated from the outside world by several inches of paper and cardboard backing. These printed words are the armor of my life. Whatever happens out there, can't happen in here. This is a world where I pick the story I want to read. I control what narrative unfolds, and if things get too sick or too scary, I can just close the cover.

I'm aware other people find this place somewhat disturbing because of the lack of stuff and things. It doesn't matter. I don't bring people to my apartment. I don't want anybody touching anything. Everything here is mine, and nobody else should ever touch it.

I do have some furniture though — a chair. It is high backed and made of some kind of dark polished wood with a sort of velvet upholstery. It is old and large and big enough to curl up in while reading. Another heirloom of someone's family, I imagine. It has a matching footrest. I also have an old wardrobe that someone tried to upcycle. That's where I keep my clothes. I don't have a lot of clothing. I wear black turtlenecks and black jeans with black boots most of the time. Occasionally, I'll wear a coat. Not having to choose outfits is another life hack I highly recommend.

Everything here is cozy and slightly old. Everything was made by somebody, not a machine. I like that. It's a quiet kind of snobbery, I suppose, but it suits me. The only modern tech I allow myself is my phone. I lose it frequently, because I do not like it very much.

Having righted myself from my fall, I crawl into bed just as dawn is breaking, and pass out for most of the day, waking around three pm.

When I open my eyes, my phone has a fuckload of missed calls and quite a few text messages.

Sitting up, I yawn and look through the messages. Annoyingly, they're happy birthday messages. My social media is set a day late, because I forgot my birthday when I put it in. Specifics and dates are not my forte, unless they relate to murder.

2

Tessie isn't in at the station when I get in. Neither is her dog. I guess she's walking him. Or maybe she's finally gone home for some sleep too. Between the two of us we are almost constantly on duty; we deserve a break.

"Holmes! Get in here!"

Or maybe not.

Chief Connor is sitting behind his desk with a death stare in his dark eyes. He's not actually angry at me, most likely. He just has a bad case of resting murder face. It doesn't help that he looks, well, almost wild. Even when he's in his dress uniform there's just something about him.

He has dark sideburns that sometimes join up with the permanent short beard he wears. My theory? He shaves in the morning, and by the time he comes in, it's already a quarter inch long. The man is *hairy*. The hair on his head is similarly dark, streaked at the temples with gray in the way everyone wishes they'll go gray, but hardly any of us actually do.

He's about forty. Or fifty. Or hell, maybe thirty. Beards make it hard to tell a man's age. I could probably find out if I was interested, but I'm not. I spend a lot of time avoiding the chief, almost as much time as I spend avoiding everybody else.

"Yes, sir?"

He emits a growl. There's no other way to say it. He makes a sound like an annoyed wolf. He picks up the paper on his desk and throws it at me, more or less. I grab it, discover it's a tabloid, and resist the urge to throw it back in his face.

"Look at the front of that."

The front page has a clearly photoshopped picture of some kind of absolute monstrosity, big, bulging red eyes and slavering jaws, the body of a man but large wings. It looks cartoonish and ridiculous. The headline and caption are worse, though. THE BROOKLYN MOTHMAN, it says. CARNIVOROUS MONSTER STALKS CITY STREETS.

I don't even need to look at the byline. I know who is responsible for this bullshit.

"Randy fucking Carrot."

"There's more detail in that article than in any of your reports."

"That's because she'll take anything anyone says and print it, after adding a bunch of her own bullshit, sir. Would you like me to make up some lies and put them in my reports?"

He growls at me, and I kind of wish I hadn't said that last sentence aloud. Chief Connor does not have time for sass or attitude. Then he says what's really bothering him. "The FBI is coming to take your case."

A grin establishes itself on my face as pure relief rushes through me. "About time!"

Chief snarls. "You're pleased to be losing a case to the Feds?"

"Sure. This thing is a mess. There's no material evidence that makes any sense, the eye witnesses are all unreliable, and somehow absolutely none of these murders have been caught on any one of the tens of thousands of security cameras in Brooklyn. The Feds have resources we don't have. If this case is going to be solved, they're going to be the ones who do it."

Chief Connor looks at me with something close to actual loathing. "We used to solve crimes, detective. Maybe you'd prefer to be on beat patrol if trying to do that is too much for you, and you just want to hand it over to big brother at the FBI."

This is about dick swinging and nothing more. Connor wants the collar to come out of the 89. Which is stupid, because nobody knows what department caught almost any criminal in the history of crime. It's petty. And, in all likelihood, it's about padding his resume for the inevitable shot at commissioner.

I don't respond to him. He's basically throwing an adult tantrum, and I'm not interested in entertaining that. I just stare at him, wordlessly, silently daring him to bust me down like he keeps threatening.

"Alright," I say, after a solid minute of mutual awkwardness passes. "Well. I am going to go now. So."

"I want this case solved before the Feds take it. You have three days."

"Alright," I repeat. I like the word alright. It could mean yes, could mean no, could mean, as it does in this case, *go fuck yourself*. "Let me get right on that."

I go to my office and close the door, pull the blinds, and check out the crossword.

Tessie gets in a few hours later. Night has fallen and Obigor is already asleep. He doesn't stir when she sets him in his little bed on her desk.

"Watch out, Chief's pissed," I say. Hopefully he's gone home. It is common knowledge that he gets twitchy around this time of the month. Almost like he has a man period.

"Well, good news for you. On the way in we got a tip. A woman has called in claiming a mothman is lurking outside her apartment."

"A mothman?"

"A man moth. A man who looks like a moth," Tessie clarifies. "Matches the description of our suspect. I was going to send units, but seeing as you're here..."

"Yeah, I'll go check it out," I sigh.

I head down to the address given. The woman lives in a third story walk-up, which makes it very unlikely that anybody is outside her window. This is Randy Carrot's fault. Once she starts publishing her bullshit there's a percentage of the population who start manifesting it in their minds.

"I saw him! I saw the mothman! I saw his beady red eyes and the blood dripping from his mouth. He was beating against my window with his wings."

I am greeted by hysteria of the kind I do not enjoy. People freaking out because something bad has happened is fine. People freaking out because they've been mind-fucked by a tabloid rag is something else.

I have to make a show of taking the woman's statement. It is consistent with the others, but that's hardly surprising given that Randy Carrot's story is sitting front and center of the tabloid she has clutched in her hand. She's seeing what she's been told to see.

"Keep your door and windows closed and locked," I tell her. It's a decent piece of advice anyway. May as well be security conscious. Just because you're paranoid doesn't mean someone can't break in and steal your shit.

"Please," she says. "Check the alley. I think he's still there."

"Alright, ma'am. I'll check the alley."

I check the alley, not expecting to see anything at all. I flash a light down there once or twice, expecting to maybe catch some rat eye shine. The shine I get back is much larger than a rat, and a lot higher up.

"The fuck?" I curse to myself. There's more than eye shine. There's a shadow that seems far too tall for my liking. There is someone down there. Someone being a real fucking asshole.

In addition to the people who start freaking out about the monsters in the tabloids, there's another group of people who get off on mimicking the monsters, scaring the shit out of the suggestible and afraid.

"Hey!" I call out. "Legs!"

I'm not going to be buying into whatever attempted horror show is about to be on display. The shadow moves and turns and comes toward me.

The tallest man I ever arrested was six foot seven. This guy has at least two feet on that guy. He's broad too. The shape of him seems odd.

This is the point where most officers would draw their weapon, but if by some bizarre chance this is a real encounter with a mothman, there's very little chance that shooting him will solve the problem.

"Yo, Halloween was last month," I call out. "Come over here, buddy. Let's talk."

His costume is very good. The closer he gets, the more the streetlight outside the alley shines on him and the more I am able to make out details. He is pale all over except for long, dark hair. I am guessing that is some kind of cosmetic effect. He's not wearing a shirt, or he wants to make it look that way. HIs body ripples with muscles that cannot be real.

What I thought was a cloak actually seems to be a pair of... wings? Nah. It's a really good cloak. Has to be. My gaze is directly distracted from the wing / cloak situation because his pale abdomen would make any bodybuilder break down and cry out of sheer, unadulterated jealousy. I cannot imagine the amount of time he must have spent sculpting and airbrushing that torso. It's a little fake-looking in how pale it is, but it does seem to move naturally, so that's interesting. He even made a second pair of arms that look a lot like the first, except they emerge lower down his torso. I guess there's a lot of silicone in there making that all look real. It's quite astonishing.

His lower body is clad in black jeans. They look as incongruous as hell. His boots are large for a man, but don't seem overly large for a whatever he's pretending to be.

Where the illusion completely falls down is around his face. He's handsome. Human handsome. Nice jaw. Good bone structure. The sort of face you see on people who are famous for being good looking, except I have no idea if he is technically good looking, because the upper part of his face has been altered with what I have to assume for sanity's sake are prosthetics and cosmetics. His eyes are a terrible red hue, and from his head, two fern-like tendrils —I'd almost call them horns — twitch and move in the slight breeze.

I am tall for a woman, 5'11. But he dwarfs me. I assume he's got stilts on under there somehow. No man is this tall naturally without having some kind of medical issue.

My training makes me check his hands. Hands. Hands. Hands are fucking everything. Where they are. What they're holding. What they're reaching for.

His hands are large, in keeping with the rest of his body. He is oddly proportionate for someone in a costume. Perhaps they are prosthetic gloves. I hope the claws are foam. If they're not, they're scimitars gleaming in the moonlight.

"Hello?" He speaks curiously and hesitantly, as if he is surprised to be spoken to.

"Buddy, dressing up the way you are is a good way to get shot. You're scaring the hell out of the neighborhood."

"Oh," he says. "That would not be good."

His voice is deep and raspy. It has a very curious quality that absolutely fascinates me. There's something hypnotic about it, an otherworldly quality.

"You're an eight foot..."

"Nine foot," he corrects me. Nothing more human than being specific about one's stats. Damn that voice. Thick. Rich. Intriguing.

"Okay, so you're a nine foot high... what would you describe yourself as?"

"Justice."

"Okay, and what's justice, to you?"

"It's my name," he says.

"Oh. I see. Justice. And how would you spell that?"

"J U S T I C E."

I'm going to guess he doesn't have any ID with that name on it. I play along. No need to get hostile yet.

"Ah, I see. And where would you say you were last Tuesday night between ten pm and five am?"

"Hm," he says. "Well. I don't generally sleep at night, so I was likely out for a walk."

"In the middle of Brooklyn in the middle of the night."

"Yes. Probably."

"I see. And while you were out for a walk did you happen to see, or perhaps do anything out of the ordinary?"

"MONSTER!" A passerby catches a glimpse of Justice, screams, and flees.

"People are dramatic here," he observes.

"You not from around here, buddy?"

"West Virginia, originally," he clarifies.

"I see. How long have you been in the city?"

"Around three months or so."

That coincides with the first murders very neatly. The beast has been stalking Brooklyn for twelve weeks exactly. It is at this point the hairs on the back of my neck start to wake up from their perpetual slumber. I don't get creeped out anymore. You see enough bits of people in various states, and you stop responding in a normal way. But this is different. This is starting to get weird.

For one, the way he moves is a little too natural. I've seen people in costumes before. There's always something awkward and wrong in the way they move. A physical stutter. He doesn't have that. When he looks around, moves his hands, takes a step, he does so like every part of him belongs to him.

"Would you mind coming with me? I have some questions I need to ask you that would be better asked in private."

I'm not going to make the mistake of trying to outright arrest him. I need to contain him, but I have no idea how I am going to get him into a cruiser. We're going to need a van.

"The night is growing old, and I am growing tired," he says. "Thank you for your interest in me, but I think I will go now."

"Stop!"

My authoritative shout rings out.

He turns around and casts a crooked grin at me.

It is at this point I realize I have not identified myself as an officer of the law. I have basically been coming across as a random strident woman.

"I do not have any money," he says. "I cannot purchase your services."

Wait. What? "Do you think I am a prostitute?"

"Are you? You're pretty enough."

"That is not the compliment you imagine it is." I produce my badge. "I am Detective Holmes. I'd like you to come in for questioning."

He shakes his head. "I can't stay, officer."

"Detective."

Now who is correcting minor details out of ego.

"I must go."

"Hold it..."

But he doesn't hold anything.

I learn suddenly, and entirely unexpectedly, that the cloak on his back is not a cloak. It is a set of large wings that open up and begin to beat at the air.

My jaw drops.

"The fuck?"

He takes off toward the moon, briefly bumping a building on the way, spiraling up into the sky. I give chase on foot, but it's not easy. His movements are hard to predict at first, but seem to be a broad spiral, which means I have to run around buildings, which means I lose him fast.

"Holy fucking..." Even as I curse to myself, I am absolutely certain that I am not fucking reporting that. I'm not putting myself in the same category as the drug addled and mentally ill. There's got to be some rational explanation for what I just saw. Holographic tech, maybe. I didn't actually touch him. Maybe the entire experience was a fancy trick of light. God knows how many tech startups are lurking in the apartments around here.

Yes. That's it. This was a trick of the light. There we go. A reasonable explanation. Thank god.

I stride into the station. Tessie is still at work. Always at work. It's too late for her ancient little dog to even bother with its usual half-demented bark.

"Tessie, can you please get me the contact information of every audio visual tech TikTok instagram social media number chan geek in a ten-mile radius."

"Uh. Why?"

I slam the table with the flat of my palm, making cups and bits of old pastry dance.

"Because someone is fucking with us. That's why."

She gives me a look over her glasses. Tessie is twenty-six years old, but she channels a much older woman most of the time. It's her penchant for thick cardigans regardless of the time of year, her perpetually messy bun, and her glasses, which I suspect have been horn-rimmed since long before that became fashionable again for some absolutely godfor-saken reason.

"I'll do what I can," she says. "But you're starting to sound like the chief. And you're starting to treat me like an assistant again. I'm not your assistant. I'm your partner."

I know I saw what I saw, but I don't know what to do with what I saw. There's madness afoot. Some kind of caper, hijinks, or conspiracy that will likely shake the foundations of what we understand humanity to be if I can't prove it to be bullshit.

At that moment my phone rings. It's Ilona.

"Tell me something sane," I say as I answer.

"I found something strange," she says. "Moth scales."

"Moth scales?"

"Yes. I suspected some kind of creepy crawly interference, and I found some powder in the wounds. I've found it before too. On the other victims, but it didn't return any immediate result. Not until I got an entomologist involved. He asked me where I got so much moth powder. It's the scales shed from the wings. Of a moth. But there's more to it. The amount of powder implies a moth of incredible size. Maybe an entirely new species."

I'm not sure what specific way I should freak out about this, so I end up standing there, staring blankly. Things are starting to come together in a way they really shouldn't, according to all laws of, well, I suppose there's not really a law against massive moth people stalking the streets of New York, but it is definitely illegal for those aforementioned moth people to murder the normies. It's always illegal to murder.

Alright. First things first. I need to find that moth again, and I need to get cuffs on him, because I am fucking not telling an FBI agent that there's a big, vicious mothman out there without said creature in custody.

How do you catch a moth?

A big light, that's fucking how.

3

Desperate times call for desperate measures. There are no official protocols for apprehending a moth-man, so I'm getting creative.

The next night, I find myself on the top of my apartment building, taping twenty hundred-thousand-lumen flashlights together, wondering if I've gone mad. If my mathematics is correct, that adds up to a total of two million lumens. Might not be the brightest thing in the city, but it's got a chance of working. I point it in the direction the last murder took place, and my last sighting of what, hell, I'm just going to call the monster.

At three in the morning, I switch my flashlight array on. Twenty buttons take some time to press, but I hammer through them all as quickly as possible, one finger pushing the buttons, the other hand on my sidearm. I'm officially afraid of this monster thing. He might not have been hostile when I talked with him in the alley, but he's left his moth scale dust all over half a dozen victims, and I have no intention of joining their number.

The light is BRIGHT. Bright enough that until I angle the array back up over the nearby buildings, I see curtains twitching in the windows across the street. Hopefully by the time they call the cops I'll be done with this mission.

I sit behind the flashlight array, cast in darkness, and I drink a beer. This is not official protocol but lying in wait on your own rooftop for a flying creature from hell to appear isn't exactly in the manual either.

The block is quiet. The city is never really fully quiet, but there are parts of Brooklyn where sleep happens. Tonight is one of those still nights, where the wind plays with loose wrappers and leaves from the few trees tolerated along the sidewalks.

It's nice out here.

I hear wings.

Holy fucking shit, **I hear wings.**

The sound of them beating nearby is enough to make me immediately wish I had not come up with this plan at all. I didn't actually think it would work, or that it would work so fast. Damn my good ideas and impeccable execution thereof.

I see him pass in front of the bright beams of light. He's even bigger than I remembered him being. When those wings are stretched out in flight mode, he seems to be at least twenty feet wide. He's a monster, in both shape and size.

I pull my gun. "Stop and surrender!"

I shout the way I was trained to shout, attempting to dominate the suspect with volume and bass. It is completely ineffective. The mothman does not care at all about my shouting, or my gun for that matter.

His arms reach out and grip me powerfully. He pulls me up against his hard body and I feel the rooftop below me abandon me entirely as I am swept up into the air.

I discharge my weapon blindly. I have no idea if I hit him or not, but I do know that he is easily able to hold onto me with three of his powerful arms while the fourth hand disarms me. I curse and start fighting. I still have my baton at my belt. I grab it out, whack it to extend it, and start smashing him directly in the face.

"Aggressive little thing," he snarls. "Stop fighting me."

I am obviously not going to do that. I am going to go down fighting. When they find my body split open like a bloody hamburger bun, they'll find bits of him with me.

His hair is long and flails out behind him, but as he slows his flight to try to deal with me, it comes whipping forward. For a brief moment, we are caught in a cocoon of his hair, his red eyes boring into mine. I am face to face with terror and death, and in this moment I feel peace. Not good peace. The dangerous kind of peace that directly precedes dying, in my experience. I don't like it when people I am trying to save get calm, and I refuse to go softly into this dark night.

I kick him where his genitals would be if he were a person.

I feel something very large. Very long. Very dangerous.

"The fuck!?"

He lets out a laugh, a sound that sends a physical chill down my spine. If that is his moth-hood, it is monstrous, just like the rest of him.

"Stop fighting me. I'm not going to hurt you."

"You've killed people! Why would I believe you!"

"It wasn't me."

"Oh, it was another massive mothman, was it?"

"Yes. My brother."

This is the kind of bullshit I hear from people all the time. People generate identical twins at an astonishing rate when they're talking to police. If I had a dollar every time I arrested some guy who said it was his brother, or some girl who said I was really looking for her sister, I'd be a thousandaire.

"You want me to stop hitting you, take me down to the ground and let me take you into the station."

"I am not interested in your human justice," he says. "Stop fighting me, or I will have to hurt you, and I do not want to."

I hit him with the baton again, of course. I'm not going to stop fighting for my life because the creature abducting me asks me to make it easier for him.

Retaliation comes swiftly. One of his big hands leaves my body and returns quickly in a harsh slap. He just fucking spanked me. Hard. His hand stays on my ass, using the grip to keep me aloft as his wings beat harder and he puts on a spurt of speed. I'd like to say that is the end of it for the thrashing, but it is not. Every time I so much as move, one of his big hands slaps my ass hard enough to make me yowl. I get the impression that he is easily strong enough to hold me with just one of his hands, so the other three are free to hold, and grip, and roam, and punish.

He snugs me tight against his body, and again I feel that thick and insanely long thing beneath his pants, pressing against my belly.

There comes a moment, when you are so far out of your normal every day reality that you forget how to act at all. I see it a lot in people who have been the victims of crime or unfortunate circumstances. They go an odd sort of blank and start reacting on instinct rather than on common sense, or their every day routines. That is happening to me now. I am being spanked in the skies above Brooklyn, my ass thrashed first by one hand, then another, big palms whipping over my sport leggings that provide fuck all in the way of protection. It hurt from the very first slap, but now it is starting to absolutely ache, and sting at the same time.

I hear myself start to whimper. I barely recognize the sound at first. I am not a whimpering, moaning, begging sort of girl. I am tough as fucking nails, and when ex-boyfriends, yeah, more than one of them, tried to spank me in bed, I'd just laugh at them.

I am not laughing now. I am trapped against the hard body of a monster and that monster is punishing me for failing to submit to my abduction.

"OW!" I hear myself gasp. "Ow, okay, fuck!"

Those big, deep red eyes look down at me. "Learning your lesson?"

"The fuck I am!"

That's an instinctive New York response. I can't help it. But it does not help the situation at all. The monster grips me even more firmly, one arm around my back to stop me from falling, another hand clamped on the back of my neck to control my head, and the other two absolutely whipping my ass with a flurry of harsh slaps that make my flesh sting and squirm so much I feel my crotch rubbing back and forth against the hard rod of what has to fucking be his monster cock.

Then it gets worse. Then those two free hands start to peel my leggings down over my ass. I wasn't wearing underwear. Have to take a trip to the laundromat and haven't gotten around to it. So when he peels my leggings down over my hot, sore ass, he finds nothing but bare skin to spank. He does so, at least a dozen times, until I am whimpering, and hot tears are gathering at the corners of my eyes.

He's hurting me. Punishing me. He's treating me like a very bad girl who deserves to be spanked long and hard. I find myself writhing in his grasp, not holding onto him but trusting him to keep me where he wants me as those slaps rain down on my poor ass, making the skin feel tighter and nearly volcanic in heated intensity.

Just when I think I cannot take another spank, his hands grip my ass and spread my cheeks. I feel his finger swipe down low between them. He's touching me *there*. My lower lips are greased with what I have to shamefully admit is desire.

I hear a chuckle, and then his mouth opens. What extends from the interior of that oral cavity is like nothing I have ever seen or imagined before. He does not have a human tongue. Instead he has something much, much longer that unrolls out of his mouth like a party blower, but one with no perceivable end.

I squirm, horrified, but it does nothing. He has me where he wants me in the moonlit sky. I have entered his realm and now he has taken me for his own.

His tongue snakes down between us, the curled tip of it finding my clit with unerring accuracy. I let out a moan as he starts to pleasure me in the midst of my crying pain, that fuzzy, strong, monstrous tongue toying with me with all the prehensile skill of an elephant's trunk. He is feeding on the nectar of my sex.

I feel my wetness being spread around my lower lips and clit. I feel the slight tickle and then firm touch of his tongue as the furred surfaces wrap around my clit and squeeze.

"FUCK!" I curse suddenly, bucking against him. The arousal coursing through me is making it impossible for me to stay in a state of complete fear and rebellion. Instead, I find myself wanting to give into him, wanting more of this release.

He spanks me again. Harder than before, but somehow it hurts less. It makes me release more juices, though, makes me wetter, gives him more to curl that strange tongue into. He is making rough, dark, guttural sounds of enjoyment as I become his sustenance.

I am being pleasured and fed upon by a ravaging monster creature. This may be the last sexual experience I have before my death. I suppose that's technically true of all sexual experiences, but it makes this one in particular feel very intense, as if I feel every nerve ending in my body individually. His lust matches mine. It has been a long time since I let any man fumble his way around my body. The moth handles me differently.

He's pleasuring me into submission. That's what he's doing. He's stopped my struggles by overwriting my processes. I should feel cheap, or terrified, or maybe outright sick, but the way I feel as he holds me and works that talented, slick, furred tongue around my lower lips and folds is enough to make me nearly come then and there.

But the moth is not done with me, and he clearly does not intend to stop with tasting and teasing alone. No. I feel the cool air around us gusting against my heated ass and nethers as his big hands hold me open, putting my most intimate parts on lewd display.

It takes me a long moment to realize that he has unleashed his cock with his spare hands. I feel the head of it probing my soaking wet pussy, soft tendrils playing over my lips for a moment before the hard, intense thickness of his rod surges forward just as all four hands pull me down and I am filled several inches deep, as far as his monster cock will go. I breathe in a gasp, my mouth open in a silent scream.

"More," he growls, pushing deeper still. I did not know there were greater depths, but he finds the final measure of me, still with several inches of his rod remaining outside.

"Fuck!" I curse, finally giving voice to the intensity of his penetration. "Oh my fuck... what are you doing... my god... my..."

I don't know what I'm saying. It's nonsense, a blend of appealing to deities and cursing all creation out at the same time.

He's fucking me now. His four arms hold me in place as his hips pump up against me, thrusting his cock as deep inside me as I can possibly take it. I look helplessly up into his face and reach out to grasp his neck as I am sternly fucked by this absolute abomination of nature.

This isn't an act of lovemaking. It's an act of domination, and possibly punishment. He warned me to do as he said, and when I failed to obey first he deployed a hand-thrashing and now he is having me endure the sensation of my very bare and unprotected human pussy wrapped around the hard surging of his monster cock.

Flying above the city I swore to serve, I become a fuck-doll for a monster of incredible strength and absolutely zero morality. My life is in his hands, and my sex is wrapped around his surging dick. I give into the sensation, because it is so intense there is nothing else I can do. The wind whips through my hair and the stars twinkle down at me as I writhe and grind, making a spectacle of myself as I am dragged back and forth along the impossibly large length and girth of his maleness until a soul-shaking orgasm ignites at the very core of me, and I start to come on him, my pussy spasming around his cock with a death grip that not only announces my climax, but demands his seed.

I hear the roar of the creature in my ears, his arms snugging all the more tightly around my curves as he thrusts hard inside me, making my sensitive flesh give way to the final act of absolute ravishment.

His seed floods me, a biological cocktail of strange substances that wash all the way up to the very neck of my womb, his essence sinking into the core of me, his flesh becoming mine, my flesh becoming his.

He keeps me there, impaled on his cock, his cum trapped inside my captive pussy as he flies on through the night, apparently unconcerned by the question of where to land. As long as we are up here, we are separate from everything below. The laws of the world, of physics and biology themselves do not seem to apply anymore.

I am left dripping and aching, inseminated with the seed of a monster as we land in a maze of shipping containers in the middle of one of Brooklyn's industrial districts. I am not sure which one because I was too busy orgasming on the rod of a hell-beast. This has not been my most professional moment. I am making those cops in 80's action movies who blow up half the city look like reasonable employees. I've baited a dangerous criminal, I've gotten myself abducted, and now all statistical odds about second locations, etcetera, tell me I'm about to be murdered. Hard.

I glance about to try and get my bearings. It's always nice to know where one's mutilated corpse will be found. These containers do not look like they have been moved or touched in a long time. There's a lot of spider webbing around the place. Canvas canopies cover the space between them, almost as if the space was designed to provide shelter for something large. Machinery probably.

The monster holds me still until we have come to a complete halt. Only then does he let me go, and only with three hands. The fourth one stays on the back of my shirt. Jesus fuck, I just fucked this thing.

"What have you done?" I breathe the question at him. I have lost a lot of moral authority by allowing him to ravage me. Even if I didn't truly have an absolute choice in that, I lost authority when I wanted it as badly as he did. I could pretend otherwise, but the moment that curling tongue touched my clit, I was done.

"Made you more sensible, I hope," he says. He speaks to me as if my objection to being aerially abducted was unreasonable. He has a very toppy vibe to him. I noticed it when we first met, but now that I am being subjected to the disciplinary and sexual effects of that vibe, I feel it plain as day.

"You had sex with me."

"You needed to be fucked," he says plainly. "You were erratic, petulant, and aroused. I have done you a service. The least you could do is say thank you."

"Thank you for fucking me?"

"You're welcome," he says.

"I didn't..." There's no point arguing. I am embarrassing myself when what I really should be doing is pulling my pants up. I do so and am rewarded by the feeling of leggings full of moth monster seed being pressed against the sex-soaked lips of my pussy.

This is twisted. And hot. And probably sick. My mind flashes to the sudden realization that if I report this, and I will have to report this, I'll have to legally mention the fact that I had sex with the murderous moth monster.

I am in fucking deep now, literally.

I still have the baton in my hand. Shame, outrage, training, you name the reason, I raise it in a foolish attempt to regain some semblance of control over this situation. I intend to slam it down on some part of his rock hard anatomy, but he catches my arm with his upper left hand before I can crack whatever passes for a skull beneath that surprisingly glossy and soft hair.

His eyes flare with irritation as he stares down at me, our discrepancy in height making me think I should stop bothering going for the face and just go for the knee instead.

"Stop fighting," he says. "Just stop. I thought detectives were supposed to be intelligent."

"You're a flying monster who has left a trail of bodies across the city. You killed good people. People who had lives left to live. You cut them short, and..."

He lets out a sigh. "If I was the creature you believe me to be, I would have already ripped your throat out to get you to stop lecturing me. Listen, detective. I am not the mothman you are looking for."

"Yeah. It's your psycho brother dropping bodies across Brooklyn. I heard your excuse. But you also just abducted me from my home, so forgive me if I don't believe you when you tell me you're not going to kill me."

"Who is that?" The question rattles from the dark nearby, stopping me mid-argument and setting my head on a swivel.

"The fuck is that?"

The question is pointless, because what the fuck that is, is another monster. Not a moth, this time. This time, the thing emerging from the dark, tight space between the containers is a man. Sort of. Just. Maybe.

His eyes are multitudinous. They blink, one after the other at me, each and every one of them annoyed with what they see. His body, much like the moth, is all muscle. He shines bright, with a bright red stripe running down his front. His arms, again, much like the moth's, are powerful, but instead of having four arms, he has six. It's a lot of arms. He is also tall, though not quite as tall as Moth.

Neither one of us is happy to see the other. He looks at me as if I am an intruder. I look at him as if he is a monster from the depths of the human psyche.

"What happened to you two? You can't have been born this way. There's just no way."

"Rude," the spider notes. He's got a stern, stiff sort of way about him. A *don't fuck with me* vibe emanates from him like a physical forcefield, over and above the natural screaming of my senses. "I thought we agreed we weren't going to eat in the nest."

"This human can help us. She's a detective."

I'm trying to get my brain to work efficiently, but a lot has happened in a very short period of time and staring between the two of them I have to wonder if I am actually having some kind of stress precipitated mental break. If it wasn't for the fact that there's a trail of very real bodies, I'd be considering talking to someone.

I am trapped between two very large, very dangerous creatures, with only my baton to protect me. When the spider speaks, I see flashes of very sharp teeth. I clap my hand over my own mouth to stop myself from screaming. I don't want to show any signs of fear or bring attention here. Either one of those things might trigger these beasts to attack.

"Okay. How many of you are there?" I mumble the question through my hand before moving it away from my mouth. I have to get a grip on something other than a cock.

They don't answer the question at first. They are having some unspoken conversation with one another, and something in the way the moth's antennae wriggle makes me think he is telling the spider to be cool. The spider does not look like he wants to be cool, even a little bit.

The moth turns his red eyes to me. They look less hauntingly intense right now. I realize that is because night is starting to surrender to day. We are not at sunrise yet, but the edges of the sky are starting to lighten a fraction.

"I want you to help me. Us. Our kind has managed to stay largely secret for decades, because we do not visit major cities and engage in heinous crimes there."

"What is your kind, would you say, exactly?" That's a sensible question. I wish I had a pad and paper so I could take some notes, but I have nothing.

"We call ourselves the Mutated."

"Mutated. Okay. That makes sense. And, uh, you got any more information on how you came to be... thus?" I gesture my baton up and down the mothman's body.

"Science did a lot of things in the forties."

"That's an understatement, and not very technical."

"I don't understand the processes myself. I am not a genetic scientist."

"Fair."

"What I do know is that the Manhattan Project was not the only piece of groundbreaking technology that allowed humanity to redefine the bounds of its power."

"Okay, but you two are forty at most. You weren't around in the forties."

"We hatched more recently. That is true."

"A detective and a mathematician. Aren't we lucky," the spider drawls, thoroughly unimpressed. He's striking me as kind of an asshole. Then again, mothman over here was striking me as a murderer until very recently, so judgements are not easy to make when it comes to these things.

"Hatched," I say. "As in, from an egg of some kind."

"We have some human DNA spliced into the DNA of other animals. We are chimera in the strictest sense of the word, though many call us cryptid."

"You have a preference for names?"

"I already told you my name is Justice. It is my name, and my calling. That is why I have been tasked with hunting down Rage. He is the mothman you are looking for."

"Rage. Well. I'd call him messy fucking asshole. He leaves absolute carnage in his wake. The bodies we found have traumatized thousands of people."

"You let thousands of people see them?" The spider cuts in, his voice full of rattly disapproval.

"People like to share pics. They end up on the internet when they're gross or weird enough. So, probably, tens of thousands of people."

"Your internet is a bane."

"Also out of the same time period as you are, technically, no?"

"Not at all. The internet wasn't conceived of until 1983. It's brand new, in the grand scheme of things. The desperate salaciousness of the average human, not to mention their appetite for gore and cruelty, that is ancient."

The spider is waxing philosophical. I don't have time for it. I need to make it very clear the shit these two, or three, or however many there are, are in. I'm back in cop mode now, and that makes me feel much more in control.

"Here's what you've done," I tell Justice. "You've abducted a New York City Detective from her property, you've left two million lumens of flashlights burning on the roof of a residential area, and you've taken my gun. Give it back."

He doesn't give it back. I'm sure he secreted it about his person, and I am equally sure that he's not going to let me search him. I could try to search him without his consent, but I am certain that getting into the pockets of a four-armed man creature is going to be more difficult than it first appeared.

"You tried to shoot me, which, if you'd done so, would have meant we could have both fallen to our deaths. You might be a detective, but your common sense under pressure leaves a lot to be desired."

"I'll tell the chief we need more aerial combat training" I say, yes, sarcastically. "Ever occur to you that I was willing to die to ensure that I got a monster off the streets?"

The spider lets out a rasping dark laugh of derision. "So you brought back a hero. Every two seconds she's going to be sacrificing herself for something else or this or that. I am going back to bed. Be quiet out here. I need my sleep." He gives me a harsh look before smushing himself back into what really seems like a space that should be far too small for him.

"What's his name?"

"Order."

"Order, alright, okay. So these are the sorts of names people get when they join cults. Who is hatching you out and giving you these names?"

"I am not at liberty to say. My kind depends on staying secret. If it were to come to the attention of the general public... we would be destroyed. My brothers and sisters yet to be born would be wiped from existence. I will not allow that to happen. My life beyond this investigation must remain secret to you."

Challenge accepted.

"Once the sun comes up, I must hide for the day," Justice says. "But you can work during the daylight hours to apprehend my brother. He will likewise be hiding."

"Where would your brother be hiding during the day, you think? And why is he killing people?'"

"Why not? He is tired of being a freak in the dark. He claims he is powerful, and he wants to show the world."

"He could do that on any cell camera and dance-based social media site."

"He prefers murder as a means of self-expression."

"You understand that if I apprehend him — and I will be apprehending him, he will go through the human justice system. Your little secret will be out. One way or another, the existence of mothmen is going to become common knowledge."

His jaw clenches and his eyes narrow. Night is swiftly becoming day, and in this ever brightening light, his eyes are starting to look a much more wholesome and far less intimidating brown.

"I am trying to help you save lives in the city. He will kill again in a matter of days, and another innocent will have lost their life for no good reason if we do not intervene. Work with me, detective."

"I'm going to do what I can, but just so you know, this case has been taken by the FBI. They're coming in a matter of days too. At that point it will officially be federal and out of my hands."

"That cannot happen."

Now I have two oversized, growly males telling me I have to fix this problem.

"I will come and see you tonight," he says. "I know where to find you."

"I might not be home."

"I'll find you," he repeats. "Good night, detective."

"Wait."

He stops just before disappearing into the same crack in the containers the spider, Order, slipped into.

"My gun, please. If I lose it, I will be in deep shit, and you don't need me filling out endless paperwork instead of looking for Rage."

He pulls my gun out of a pocket in his pants and hands it back to me. "Be careful," he says. "Rage has no respect for life or the law. He has become unstoppable, convinced only that he deserves his vengeance against the world that created and then rejected us."

"I don't think we rejected you. People are very understanding and respectful of a lot of things these days. Maybe you should try coming out of the shadows."

"That is not permitted," he says. "We cannot show people how tenuous and conditional their humanity is, how close they are to beasts, and how a few shifting molecules can change what they are from the inside out. People like to feel certain in their own existence. They like to know what kind of animal they are. We threaten that."

He speaks eloquently, but I have the feeling that the words coming out of his mouth aren't really his. If they've never come in contact with people before, at least on a wide scale, then they don't really know how they would be received at all.

"Who told you that?"

"It doesn't matter."

"It does, actually. You want me to find your murderous brother, and you've given me two-tenths of fuck all in terms of actual information. To catch a criminal, you have to understand a criminal. I have approximately 72 hours to achieve this, and you're refusing to help."

"I can tell you that he likes red lights."

"Red lights."

With that, Justice disappears between the containers in a motion that is equally mysterious and awkward. I wonder what's in there? Are they just squishing themselves away like bugs do? Or do they have some kind of container-based monster clubhouse? I must know.

4

The asshole has basically stranded me. Fortunately by some act of magic or luck I do still have my phone on me.

One uncomfortable and surprisingly sticky uber ride later, I am in my apartment, showering moth cum from my inner thighs and wondering what I am doing with my life. I have never slept with a suspect. I have also never encountered a flying criminal, so maybe I need to give myself some slack.

It was hot. It was wrong. It was supernatural.

I can't stop thinking about Justice. It feels like he is the only thing I am going to think about for a very long time. *Justice.* What a name. Almost poetic. He stopped looking quite so weird once the sun came up too. It's funny how quickly you can start to get used to something odd once you, well, fuck it.

The idea of a race of mutants created by Second World War scientists makes sense. Ethics weren't exactly anybody's priority at the time. I wonder how many they are, and I wonder how living disenfranchised and afraid of general society has caused them to either be afraid, or in Rage's case, apparently murderously angry.

First, I need to make sure that there is actually a second moth creature. Justice produced no evidence for one. As for having slept with me, he admitted he did it just to stop me fighting him. There's a manipulative, or perhaps simply outright controlling streak in him. It wasn't that he was overcome with love. It's that he wanted something and figured the fastest way to get it was sex.

And spanking.

When I turn around and the hot water hits my ass, I am painfully reminded of the fact that he punished me in his own way, brought me to his version of justice.

The physical anomalies are not the only differences between the mutants and normal humans. Justice has a dominant way about him, and clearly some small amount of respect for the ways of greater society, because he asked for my help. Hell. Maybe he even respects me?

"You got laid!"

Tessie erupts with the words when I walk into the station. I glance around to see if anybody heard. Most of the officers present seem to be busy with work, but they have functioning ears.

"I have no idea what you're talking about."

"Oh my god," she hisses. "You slept with someone you shouldn't have. Who was it? Was it Roger from the 73?"

"You are not going to guess," I tell her. "And please, stop talking right now. The last thing I need is office gossip. There's always someone around here listening."

"Oh my god," she whispers more quietly. *"It was someone really bad. Was it your ex?"*

"No, Tessie, sex detective, it was not. I have a lead on the case. I'm going to do some work. Is that alright with you?"

"Maybe you didn't get laid," she says, narrowing her eyes suspiciously. "Something is going on with you, though, I can sense it."

Something is definitely up with me.

I look at the scene photos. Not the ones of the body, but the ones of the surrounds. Justice gave me practically no help besides the mention of Rage liking the color red, and presumably as a mothman, red lights.

I immediately notice that across the street from the murder scene is a discount store with a big glowing red sign with a perpetual 50% off logo on it. Then, on either sides of the alley, there's a liquor store and an appliance center. Both of them have bright neon lighting.

"Well, fuck," I murmur to myself, going back over previous scene images. I quickly find that in each and every case, there's a discount store location with one of the big, round signs. Red Light Discount, they call themselves.

I should have picked up on that earlier. We all should have, but this case has been distractingly gory and who links murders to discount chain stores. We looked at the victims, mostly male, mostly of a strong build. We thought there might be some connection between them somehow, because when a human serial killer kills, his victim profile is quite often revealing.

Now I am starting to wonder if the only thing in common these people had was looking like a good meal and happening to walk past an alley opposite one of these Red Light Discount locations. We were looking for a human, with a human killer's motivations. Instead, we're looking for what might as well be an animal, hunting and killing.

I return to the scene of the most recent crime, a sad and filthy alley which extends the entire block, very narrow. It's a choke point, and the sort of place most people avoid because it's the sort of place one could easily be stabbed. The scene has been opened up to the public again, but it's quite obviously not the sort of place people want to hang out. It smells of piss and worse things besides.

Is this really where the murderer is? Is he so arrogant as to stay near his last meal, slowly digesting the better parts of an unlucky son of a bitch?

Holy shit.

I see him.

Behind some rancid dumpsters, pressed against the filthy wall, wings out, the back of his head nearly flat with the building, he's easy to miss. In the same way moths are camouflaged when they land on trees, he is camouflaged against the filthy brick alley wall. It makes me wonder if these creatures don't have some ability to shift their appearance like a chameleon. That would have been useful to hear from Justice.

Rage the murderer must have been here the entire time, throughout the scene examination, while I was here with my party hat on. He was no doubt listening to our conversations, probably laughing at us as we expressed how grossed out we were.

I am not sure what to do. Having found a mothman is one thing but apprehending him is something else. I keep walking, not wanting him to know that I've found him. He probably can't see behind his head, but I am sure he has some form of chimera awareness of his surroundings.

I could go and get Justice, but he can't emerge during the day, and I can't risk letting this criminal murderer go. So fuck it. I retreat from the alley, and I call for backup. "As many units as possible, converging on last murder location. No sirens. No lights. Take it easy. Suspect is asleep in the alley."

Within ten minutes, there are six cruisers, three on each end of the alley. With a normal criminal, this would be the kind of pincer maneuver that helps us ensure there is no route of escape. I'm not so sure how it's going to work with this kind of criminal. I never tried to catch a mutant before.

"Is the suspect armed, detective?"

"I don't know. I just know he's in there. Behind the dumpsters."

I should tell them that he's an eight foot plus moth, but my mouth refuses to form those words. I keep hearing them out of other people's mouths in my mind, and I can't be one of those people who says those things.

The officers approach from each side, guns drawn. I don't know why they are bothering. In this tight an alley, facing one another, there's a far better chance of shooting each other than there is of getting the monster.

I'm starting to feel guilty as they approach the spot I found Rage. I know that what is about to happen is going to change their lives forever. Any moment, they are going to come face to face with a creature unlike any they have ever seen, and I won't be crazy when I talk about a mothman.

The officers reach the middle of the alley together and look around, clearing the area.

"We've got nothing. You sure you had a guy here?"

"He was up against the wall."

"Well. There's nobody here." They look at me like I've wasted their time, which I suppose I have. I go down the alley and look for myself. They're right. There's absolutely nothing there whatsoever.

The uniformed officers are confused. I am confused.

"Alright, well."

It's awkward now.

The officer makes a thumb jerk gesture in the direction of his car. "We'll get going. Let us know if you see any other murderers."

I am left looking and feeling like a complete asshole. I walk the length of the alley and back to the spot he was. They're not wrong. It's just normal wall. I'm left wondering if I was wrong, if I ever saw him at all.

And then I look up. Above my head, he is splayed across the distance between two buildings, four arms and two legs pressed against the bricks on either sides. He is looking down at me with a broad, self-satisfied grin, and before I can so much as shout, he winks one red eye and flaps his wings, skittering up onto the roof.

"ASSHOLE!"

I give chase, up the liquor store, through the back, and then up the fire escape. I am not going to let him go. I am not going to let any moth asshole make me look stupid. I'm going to go up there, and I'm going to bring him down.

I burst up onto the roof, panting and with my gun drawn. Just as I figured, he's on the roof. He can't leave the roof without flying, and he can't fly in daylight without exposing himself to more New Yorkers than we can count.

Up close, he looks a lot like his brother, but in an angrier, more murderous kind of way. Red eyes give themselves to a kind of natural intimidation. This is a scary motherfucker. His wings are jet black now. His clothes are simple. Blue jeans and boots. That's it. He's naked from the waist up, and his chest looks smooth and I'd say hairy, but it's probably furry. The hair is dark brown, but I suspect he can change and shift that too. He's different from Justice. His upper lip is curled back in a perpetual snarl, and I can see that his teeth are both sharp in some places, and flat and chew-ready in others. It suddenly makes sense why the bite patterns were so odd in the victims. It also makes it readily apparent that he ate them raw.

"You shouldn't have come up here," he says, seething visibly. His shoulders are rising and falling with deep breaths. It must take some effort to do a plank twenty feet above ground while half a dozen cops are searching for him.

"You shouldn't have murdered a bunch of people. What did you think was going to happen?"

"Ugh," he grunts. "I had to eat. What did you want me to do?"

"Get a slice, man. Eat literally anything besides people."

He starts advancing toward me. "You'll be my next meal."

I deploy my taser. Forty-two thousand volts hit him, and he goes down like a fucking sack of twitching shit, his wings moving in what looks to me like uncomfortable and unnatural ways.

Serves him fucking right.

I came here prepared. I have two sets of handcuffs, and I get them on both sets of wrists, cuffing him in the front. I'd usually go around the back, but the wings are in the way. I start reading him his rights before he stops twitching.

"You have the right to remain silent. Anything you say can and will be used against you in a court of law."

"Let me go. You can't take me into your station."

"Why not?"

"I'm not human."

"You're human enough to speak English."

"I'll kill everybody I come into contact with. I'll turn your precious station into a bloodbath. And it will be your fault."

"Oh god." I crouch down next to him. "Do you think you're the first violent murderer I've encountered? You think your threats are original? Interesting? I don't give a fuck if you're a moth. You're going to jail."

His mouth opens, and I see inside his maw. Just behind his lips, there is a second set of surfaces pulsing hungrily, serrated cartilage and flesh. These must be the mouthparts Ilona was talking about. They're gross, and they're even more evidence, if I needed it, that I have the right flying man-monster in custody.

I call for backup. Again. This time, I am triumphant. I have overcome the monster. It's all going to be okay.

"I've got him. I need a van and at least two units."

There's a brief pause from the dispatcher, who is far too professional to mention that I just called a few minutes ago and it led to nothing.

"Units on the way. Van en route."

"You hear that, murder buddy? In a few minutes you'll be nice and cozy in your very own cell, answering for the many crimes you've committed."

"I can smell Justice's seed on you," Rage growls. "He always had a taste for stupid women. I think it makes him feel better about his own limited intellect."

I let him talk shit. This time I've got him. This time there's no way he's getting away. Two sets of cuffs mean he's not going fucking anywhere. I stand next to him, making sure he stays in one piece until backup arrives.

"What brings you all out here anyway? Can't say we've seen your kind before."

"Oh, you've seen our kind before," Rage laughs. "You call them unsolved mysteries or urban legends. I am far from the first to give into the instinct to feed on you normies."

"Normies?"

"Normal people. Cattle. Sheep. Humans. All the same thing. Underdeveloped. Undesigned. You're produce, like lettuce. Nature made you lesser things to serve a higher purpose."

This creature has an ego that will not quit.

"So this is like some kind of toxic cannibalism you're into, huh?"

"Cannibalism is when you consume your own species. I am not of your species."

"Okay, so why come to a city where you're going to be noticed? Why not stay out in the woods of ass-fuck nowhere and pick off people without creating a federal investigation?"

"Why do your kind go to a bakery instead of foraging in a desert? The food is just better here."

There is a disturbing logic to this human smorgasbord theory he has developed.

"You know, Justice is very angry at you, and Order, the spider."

"They are weak. Secretly they want to consume just as I do. Order's web is capable of catching dozens of your kind, and he would make such a pretty meal of you all, sucking the delicate juices from your flesh, veins, and bone. Dammit."

"Dammit what?"

"I'm making myself hungry," he complains.

"You're a piece of work, buddy," I say. I've heard worse, unfortunately. People who break the law in heinous ways tend to have pretty awful things to say to you once they're caught. It's like a release valve is opened, and all the foul thoughts that have been motivating them through their crimes suddenly come pouring out. It's actually very human of him to be giving me this fucked up little speech of his.

Heavy boots are coming stamping up the stairs. In less than a minute, I am going to be the detective who collared the first actual monster on the force.

"Hear that, my guy? Once they get here, it's over for you. You're going to be taken to a human police station, charged with crimes against humans, and subsequently judged and sentenced, one way or another."

"No. I won't. I'll be taken into custody, and then I'll be disappeared, tortured, murdered, and my parts put on display."

He might not be wrong. There's no way a mothman is going to go through the standard court system unimpeded. Every government and military agency is going to want a piece of him, maybe literally. Can't say I feel sorry for him. After what he did to his victims, he deserves what's coming to him.

He's been lying on his back all this time, looking up at me with those ferociously cruel eyes and oddly shaped teeth bared at me. As the door to the roof swings open, he beats his wings. They bring him up from the roof like a jack in the box. He just pops up right into my face and I realize I have underestimated him by a lot. He wasn't subdued. He was resting.

For a brief moment I am face to face with him. He laughs at my shocked expression, winks at me, and is fucking gone. He flies fast, like an arrow shooting skyward straight up into the sky.

How the hell did I forget about the wings? I assumed he wouldn't risk flying in front of people, but he takes off vertical, heading straight up as fast as he can, and before I know it he's a speck in the sky.

Two officers emerge from the roof door. They're older, heftier, and they don't look impressed at having to run up the stairs, if they even ran. They do not look happy to see me standing there without anything vaguely resembling a suspect. I wanted so badly not to come out of this looking like a fucking idiot, but here I am, idioting as hard as anybody ever idioted.

"Where's the perp?"

"I had him. Uh."

"Where is he?" The other cop asks the question again, because I have failed to answer.

"He flew away. I mean." I have to come up with a story, and fast, because they're getting that look on their faces that tells me they think I am fucking with them. "He just fucking jumped. Just as you opened the door, he ran with the cuffs on and leaped."

They walk to the edge of the building. I walk too, pretending the lie is true.

"It's a long way down to not break a leg," one officer notes.

"People on drugs make taller jumps than this and survive. At least, far enough to get away," I say.

"We're going to need a description for the search," the older officer sighs. They're from another precinct, as most cops are. They're giving me looks that tell me I am going to be the talk of every cop shop in the vicinity. I start rattling off information.

"Male. Eight feet tall. Shirtless. Jeans."

A brow is raised at me. "Eight feet tall?"

"Maybe seven."

The officer is an older man, white mustache, and no time for this bullshit. He drops his pad and looks at me askance. "Alright, detective, what's going on?"

"He's an oddly shaped creature... person."

"How odd?"

"Very odd. He's costumed. He has wings. And..."

I can't believe those words just came out of my mouth. Wings. Fucking wings. The number of times I rolled my eyes when people told me about the wings.

"Like the itty bitty butterfly wings little girls wear? Is he jacked on something and dressed up, or?"

"More like oversized moth wings."

"Detective…" He pauses and breathes. "Alright. Moth wings, no shirt. I'll let the boys know."

"Thank you. I'm sorry I lost him."

"Hey," he says. "It happens. Don't worry about it. Maybe time to clock off, once you've written your incident report. You look… pale."

I know what he really means. I look fucked up. Like a tweaker junkie. Like the poor bastards I've been judging this whole time.

The paperwork might very well be the most punishing part of this job. I suppose I deserve some kind of penalty for smugly forgetting Rage had fucking wings. I'm not used to thinking of vertical escape potential, and the adrenaline of having caught the monster overrode my sense. I shouldn't be out here alone. I should have a partner, but of course being in the freak unit, it's practically mandatory to demand to work alone. I compromised by taking on Tessie as a partner.

I go back to the station. It's so good to see Tessie and her ancient dog Obigor there. Obigor is chewing on something soft for his aging teeth, and Tessie is chewing on something that looks remarkably similar.

I shut the door very quietly, close all the blinds, go sit at my desk, and park my forehead between stacks of paperwork.

"That good, huh?"

"I caught him. It. Whatever. I caught him and he got the fuck away."

"That happens," Tessie says, sympathetic. "You caught him once, you'll catch him again."

"Technically, I caught him twice and lost him twice. He's got two pairs of handcuffs on, for fuck's sake."

"Then you've got precedent for finding him again."

She's so encouraging. I appreciate that.

I lift my head to look at her. "I need to tell you something, Tessie."

"What's that?"

"He does have wings. He is a mothman. With wings and burning red eyes."

There's a long pause in which she is probably trying to work out if I have had a break from reality. "At least the eyewitness reports were accurate?"

"They were," I say. "They really were. He's going around killing people for food. He feeds on us like... like cattle feed on grass. He hates us, and he wants to consume us."

"The more I hear about this guy, the more he sounds like a real jerk," Tessie says. "You want some candy?"

"I'm not hungry. Not after... and I can't talk to my informant until the sun goes down."

"Alright," Tessie says. She gets up from her desk and walks over to mine. She has a limp that's worse some days than others. If she has to go further than the office, she uses a suitably dramatic walking stick with a sapphire tip.

"Listen," she says. "I need to know. Are you losing your mind? It's okay if you are. I lost my mind once, and it wasn't as bad as you'd think it is, though it was also not great."

"I wish. But this is real. There are at least two mothmen, and a spiderman."

"Uh huh." She frowns. "I'm really not sure what to do with this information."

"Me neither. One of them flew away with two sets of cuffs on him."

"Those things are not cheap," she says, cheerfully missing the point in the way people do when they don't want to pay attention to what you're actually saying because then they'll either have to join your madness or refute it, and neither option appeals. I've been where she is before. I wish I was still there.

"I have to show you," I tell her. "You're my partner, and you should know. You should see this."

"You're right," she says after a brief moment of struggling with the notion of what I'm asking. "But if it involves going outside, I'd rather not."

"We can take your car," I tell her. "That's a kind of inside."

"Alright," she says, frowning. "But only because this is an emergency."

5

Tessie's car is a nifty little bubble-shaped thing with a faded red paint job. It's the sort of car that annoys people in parking lots because they think a space is open, but nope, Tessie is there. She has disabled parking tags because of her gunshot injury, and a special carseat for the dog in the front passenger seat. That means I'm stuck in the back of the car with my knees up to my chin.

When we get to where we're going, things have changed. There is now a large web strung out all the way in front of the pair of shipping containers that bookend their little hidey-hole. Ordinarily, I'd be creeped out by the sight of such a massive web, but because I'm now passingly familiar with the creature who made it, it's now even more creepy.

"What kind of fucking spider made that?" Tessie exclaims.

"The annoyed kind that doesn't like people very much," I say.

"It's getting dark," Tessie comments. She looks uncomfortable. I don't blame her.

"They don't come out in the daytime."

Tessie glances over at me with suspicious brown eyes. "Listen. I thought..."

Before she can finish her sentence, Obigor starts barking ferociously, snarling and yapping with hackles raised. He is facing the wrong direction entirely, but I appreciate his effort.

"Alright. So. What are we looking for? This doesn't feel like a terribly inhabited sort of place."

"Just wait. We need to get around this thing..."

I start trying to clear away the spider web. This, I quickly discover, is a Very Big Mistake. Normal spider webs are slightly sticky and somewhat gather up together in a gooey kind of way when you put your hand through them. The fibers of this web are about double the thickness of a typical one, and they are much, much stickier. It is like having put my hand into some spun goo, a sort of biological slime. When I try to pull it away, it does tear a little, but it also gets tangled around my hand.

"Ah, fuck!"

I lift my leg, I don't even know why, it's kind of a pulling away reflex, but somehow my toe gets caught in the lower part of the web, and then my knee. I put my full weight against the webbing, but all that happens is a brief low bounce and then a rebound which sticks a lot more of me to the strands. I twist myself to try to get free, which only succeeds in getting me more wound up as fresh bits of web stick to new parts of my body.

Tessie is watching me with what I'm just going to call a dour and unimpressed expression. Obigor is still barking in the wrong direction. I continue to fight the web, worsening my situation until I am nearly entirely upside down at a 45 degree angle.

"Are you alright?" She asks the question more as a formality than anything. Clearly I am not alright. Not even remotely.

"Tessie?"

"Yes."

"What are you doing?"

"Nothing."

She lies directly to my face. She has her phone out and I am 99.999% sure she is filming my predicament.

"Don't fucking put that on social media," I warn her. "I don't give a shit how many likes you might get for it, this is top secret."

"Oh, so, live-streaming this would be a problem?"

I'm pretty sure she's kidding, but just in case she isn't, I pull the fingers. Both hands. Only one of them can really be seen from her angle.

"Fucking help me, Tessie."

"How am I supposed to help you?" She asks the question very practically. "Does me getting trapped in the same web help you somehow?"

"JUSTICE!" I yell for the mothman.

"I think this kind of is justice," Tessie says, grinning. She doesn't know his name. She just thinks I am crying out for the concept of the thing. This is what happens when you don't communicate well with your partner.

"What are you doing?" The question raps from the darkness that has gathered around the shipping containers. It is night, and the monster has risen.

Not the one I want, though. Justice is not here. Instead, it is Order who speaks from the darkness.

"Tessie, you're about to see something really fucking weird," I tell her. "Put your phone away, and don't freak out."

I'm so glad to see her listen. We do not want pics of these creatures. I don't want them being uploaded to the cloud somewhere and ending up hacked or just found when they're trawled through by the half a dozen agencies free to sift through private data as and when they please.

"I knew you were trouble," Order says, emerging from the darkness in a slow strolling gait. "I told Justice you'd be back. And that you'd be looking for trouble."

"So you set a web trap for me?"

"The only way to be trapped by a web is to walk into it," he growls, displeased. He's getting closer now, and the rising moon is highlighting him in all his six-armed glory. He's still wearing his sunglasses, the mirrored surfaces hiding what must be an absolute plethora of eyes. His jaw is hard and strong, clenched because he's annoyed.

I can only imagine the way Tessie is reacting to seeing this strange man-creature emerging from the depths of the night. Each of his pairs of arms are engaged in a different activity. The lowest pair hang loose, the middle pair are rubbing together, in a way that strongly puts me in mind of a man about to indulge some punitive urges. The top two are clapping sarcastically as he approaches me, trussed up in what I have to assume is his butt silk.

"What the fuck," Tessie breathes. Obigor has fallen silent. I glance over at him and see that he's actually gone to sleep in her arms. It's hard being an ancient tiny dog. You can only bark the alert for so long before you need a nap.

Order's many eyes have not missed her. "You brought someone. With a sick, small animal and a limp."

"Fuck off," Tessie snaps. "He's not sick. He's just old."

Order looks skyward. "Is every human in this city so rude?"

"Listen, buddy, you can insult me all you want, but Obigor is perfect and beyond reproach. Get it?" Tessie is strident, stern, and apparently completely unbothered by the strangeness of Order.

"What is wrong with your leg?" He walks around me, leaving me dangling awkwardly as a third wheel.

"Leave her alone!" I utter the order knowing that there's no chance he's going to listen to me.

As I expected, I am ignored.

"I was shot," Tessie says, blunt as always. She doesn't seem scared of him, though she has to be shitting herself. I see her rock back slightly, as if she's thinking about taking a step away from him. She chooses not to though, and instead stands her ground as he comes to stand over her, his strange form looming over her and Obigor.

"Is someone going to get me the fuck out of here?" I raise my voice. I am starting to get impatient with my captivity.

"Detective?"

Finally, Justice arrives. And when I say arrives, I mean he squeezes out of the gap between the containers. He does not seem surprised to find me trapped in the web.

"Can you get me down, please?"

He ignores the request and instead asks me a question.

"Have you come with news?"

"I'll tell you what I have to tell you when you let me down out of here. It's an offense to set traps for officers of the law, by the way."

Justice puts all four of his hands on his hips, or just above them, and peers down at me with narrowed red eyes. He seems taller than ever from this nearly inverted position.

I feel like I am in trouble, which makes no sense. I am the one who tells other people that they are in trouble. I do not get in trouble myself.

"You want the bad news, or the worse news?"

His eyes narrow even further in a serious way. "Tell me what has happened."

"I found him, tased him, cuffed him, and then he flew away."

I turn my gaze from him to check on Tessie. Before I can see her, my chin is grasped and my face is gently, but firmly directed so I am looking at Justice.

"So he is flying about with his hands cuffed?"

"Presumably. Or maybe not. He seems like the resourceful kind. Look. Let me down from here. This is starting to become obnoxious."

"I agree," he says firmly.

"HELP!"

I hear Tessie squeal. Obigor barks. They both share the same pitch of shrill outrage and fear.

I renew my struggles, which, as before, only serves to get me even more stuck in Order's web. I can just barely see where she was standing. She is gone. Obigor is gone. Order is gone. I see her walking stick lying on the ground. As I watch, one of Order's limbs comes briefly into my limited field of vision to snatch it up.

"What's he doing to her? Let her go!"

"I need reassurance that you will not attempt to take my brother into your custody. I believe that is what you intended to do, and I will not tolerate it. I need you to help me, detective. I do not need for you to help yourself."

"Fuck you. Let me out of here, and give Tessie back, or I swear to god, I will have both of you freaks inside a cell before you can say giant can of insect spray."

Justice lets out a grim chuckle. "You're impertinent and your threats are ill-advised. I think I will let you dangle a little longer, detective, until you come to terms with who is in charge here."

Oh, this asshole is really annoying me now. "If any harm comes to Tessie, or her dog, I will not stop. I will destroy the both of you."

"She is in no danger."

"She's been abducted by a massive human spider!"

"He won't hurt her. Probably. You should have known better than to bring us a hostage."

"I thought we were on the same side."

"We are not. We are on very different sides. It's just that for the moment, our interests align."

"I'm going to give you fair warning," I say, swinging lightly in the breeze with the momentum of the web set in motion by my struggles. "I am not the girl you want to be fucking with on this."

Justice laughs, reaches out, and spanks my upturned ass. Hard. I didn't notice that I'd somehow put myself in the perfect position to be punished, but there's no denying that my bent, trapped knees present the rounds of my rear for his discipline almost as perfectly as if it were intentional.

His slap makes me squirm and makes the web shake. I am once again set swaying back and forth. Justice takes full advantage of that, slapping my ass, letting me swing away, and then smacking me again when I swing back.

"The fuck! What are you doing?"

"Punishing you for your rudeness, your ineptitude in catching my brother, and your attempt to incarcerate him."

"But... you weren't there. How am I supposed to catch someone with wings? I can cuff him all I like, he's always going to be able to fly away. And.. oW! Cut that the fuck out!"

He does not cut it the fuck out. He spanks me until my ass is throbbing and sore as hell, and I am feeling both pissed off and very sorry for myself. I no longer feel like helping him, that's for sure. I want to see him behind bars for assaulting an officer.

I want him to respect me. I want him to treat me like a person of authority. But he clearly doesn't see me that way. To Justice, I am nothing but a pawn to be used and punished if I fail to serve to his satisfaction.

This was the last thing I expected to have happen tonight. I thought he might be slightly miffed at what happened, but this is... he's treating me like a servant who failed to please her master.

"You need to be more careful," he lectures. "You walked into the web the moment you saw it, and you brought a friend with you in a very delicate condition. She could have been greatly harmed if you had encountered a hostile beast."

"You are a hostile beast! And she's been kidnapped."

"Don't worry about her. Worry about yourself, brat."

"Brat!" I repeat his comment, offended. How dare he. "I am an officer of the law. I am a detective of the New York City

Police Department. I bring down murderers. I protect people. I am not a fuckin' brat."

"Yes," he says, steadying me briefly, only so he can spank my ass harder. He then continues lecturing me as I bounce back and forth in the net, yowling. "You are. You hide behind the law you claim to serve in order to do as you please."

"The fuck?" The accusation maybe isn't that far off, sometimes, but he doesn't know me well enough to know that. I haven't done anything wrong. "I went and found your psycho brother like a goddamn criminal courier. It's not my fault my tools don't cover winged perps!"

"Yes. I intended to help you with a tool for that."

"Maybe you should help me instead of lecturing me and punishing me for not catching a monster by myself in less than twenty-four hours. Christ, even my chief is more reasonable than you!"

My ass fucking hurts and my ego is bruised. I am also very, very worried about Tessie and Obigor. I don't trust Order as far as I can't throw him.

"The net you stuck yourself in within seconds of seeing it is not for you," Justice says to me. "It's for my brother."

"Oh. That makes sense."

"Yes. Now all we need to do is lure him into it and we will be able to take care of him."

"How? You've obviously lost control of him. You're sending me rushing about the place without the slightest bit of help, just vague clues. Now you're suddenly interested in helping and keeping him under control? He has killed thirteen people! He needs to pay the price for that. I'm not handing him over to you so you can...FUCK!"

Another harsh slap lands on my ass. This one, coming on top of the previous several dozen, hurts like Hades.

"He will be incarcerated," Justice says. "He will serve his sentence."

"What sentence? He'll get life in prison, and he's lucky the death penalty was rolled back here."

"He would be confined somewhere he could no longer do harm. We take killing humans very seriously. We know how precarious our position is in this world, how quickly we could be eradicated if our existence was to be discovered. This is a matter of survival for us all. Now. Are you ready to come out of there and do some work?"

"I've been working all day, asshole."

He sighs softly. "So that's it."

"That's what?"

"You like being punished. Are you jealous of the criminals you catch, because they get to be in trouble, while you have to be a good girl? Is that why you cause trouble for your chief?"

"The fuck are you talking about?"

I love being from New York. It makes cussing someone out feel more like a cultural experience than actual rudeness.

"I'm talking about the way you keep challenging me, and the way you insist on earning punishment even while you are earning punishment. You never do anything simply or easily. And you are careless."

"I am not! What makes you say that?"

"Aside from the fact you are currently upside down in a web, you left a bank of high lumen lights on the roof of your apartment.

"I did?" I think a second. "Oh, shit. I did."

"I turned them off," he says. "Before you set your building on fire."

"Thanks," I say. I am now almost becoming accustomed to this strange position. The blood moving away from my ass helps it cool down faster, I think. Or maybe the blood rushing to my head makes me too dizzy to really care. Either way, I've convinced myself I'm winning, though I am still upside down and captive.

"Order!" Justice calls out. "Can you free this human, please?"

The spider sighs as he re-emerges. "Must I? She has done very little to assist us, besides bringing a hostage, and that was hardly intentional."

"What's wrong with your hand?"

"The dog bit me."

"Yes! Good work Obigor! Let them go, you sicko!"

This outburst is unprofessional. Maybe Justice is right. Maybe I do need to really look at myself and the way I comport myself among the monster people of the world. Maybe if I was just a little more formal, they might not be psychopathic creatures directly out of the nightmares of the common consciousness. Or maybe it doesn't matter at all how I talk, because their agenda is darker and stranger than anybody can possibly imagine.

"Please," Justice says. "Unless you want her company all night long?"

That's enough to convince Order to set me free. He approaches me at what has to be an undignified angle for me, because everything about this situation is undignified for me. His spider crotch is quite close to my face for a moment. I catch a scent of something I don't think I should be smelling. It smells like Tessie has been having a good time there. No. That can't be possible. She wouldn't dry hump a spider monster within minutes of being abducted. Tessie barely likes to talk to anybody, let alone rub on them.

"What have you been doing to my partner?"

Order chuckles under his breath but doesn't deign to reply. He focuses instead on getting me down.

He does so by unsnapping the webbing from around me with palms that must be made of a special substance, because it doesn't stick to him, or he to it. I guess it's like you can't taste yourself, or something.

When the last strand snaps, I'd have fallen onto my head but for the fact that Justice grabs me by the leg and prevents the top of my skull from cracking against the concrete.

"Lucky save," I grin up at him.

"Lucky for you, perhaps, human. I am not so certain." He continues to hold me by my ankle, much like the way a fisherman might hold a fish he's thinking of throwing back.

"Listen. I found your brother."

"And spooked him."

"I doubt that. He seems like too much of an asshole to spook. Way too convinced he's right about everything. I bet he doesn't give a shit."

"I need to be able to trust that you won't try to put him in prison."

"I am literally an officer of the law. I am definitely going to try to put him in prison."

"We've had this discussion."

"Yes. We have."

"You know we have your partner. When you catch him, and I am sure you will because you are that kind of irritant, you will call me. I have a cell phone."

"You didn't want to give me your number last night? Or were you planning on us being more of a one-night flight sort of thing? You made me do the Uber of shame today. That wasn't cool. I'm starting to think that being a selfish jerk might just run in whatever passes for your family."

He reaches down with his lower left arm and hauls me up, letting the grip on my leg go so I swing around and end up back on my feet in front of him. I find myself rubbing my ass furiously, trying to get the sting out of it.

"You have got to stop that," I tell him. "It's causing a problem in our working relationship."

"My brother will have been enraged by your actions today," he says, casually. "He will likely take it out on someone innocent. Instead of asking for less of the punishment you deserve, why don't you accompany me on the hunt."

"Happy to. Let's get this murderer off the streets, one way or another. And get Tessie back. He better not be doing anything to her she doesn't want to have done to her. And Obigor, the continuation of the world as we know it hinges on the welfare of that dog. Do you understand me?"

"I understand you're yapping when you should be hunting."

Alright. Asshole. "I have an idea of where he might be. He likes the discount store signs. They're red and obnoxiously bright. I'm guessing he would have had to go somewhere to remove the cuffs, and once he removed the cuffs, he'd be off to the nearest Red Light Discount to kill someone.

"So. Where would you go to get cuffs removed?"

"Hm."

"Hmmm."

"Huh."

A lot of detecting is just standing around thinking. We don't know where he went, and we may not know until a fucking body shows up. I'm thinking about where a guy with four arms might be able to get his cuffs hacked off right now, assuming he went and hid away from the light again.

"A factory," I say. "Spinning blades. That's what he needs. Or something sharp. Or blunt. Or hard."

"Or he needs the key," Justice says, speaking slowly and clearly as if I am missing the point.

"But I have the key."

"Exactly."

"Oh. Fuck. No. I see where you're going with this. There's no way I am going to be held out as bait."

"Either you are bait, or he finds other food."

"Not with his hands cuffed together, he won't. It's going to be a lot harder for him to hunt. I might very well have saved a lot of lives tonight."

"You'll save even more when you give him the key."

"He's not going to be able to find me, though, is he?"

"He is, because I am going to call him, tell him that I have the human he crossed today in my custody, and that she will unlock him if he turns himself in."

"That's.... He's not going to go for that."

"Why not?"

"Because he doesn't want to just be unlocked. He wants flesh and vengeance. God. Have you ever baited a murderer before? Tell him he can eat my face right off. Give him a little something to look forward to. Tell him you're gonna slice me up and share me around like a sushi platter. Tell him I just ate sushi."

I am getting into this a little too much, but once the creativity starts, it just doesn't stop.

"There's something wrong with you," Justice says after a very long pause, the kind of pause in which intense judgements form.

"There's not. You do the work I do, see the things I do, you either get used to them and start talking about them real casually, or you stress the fuck out and they cart you away. So. Tell your crazy cannibalistic brother that you have a hundred sixty pounds of prime meat here waiting to uncuff him."

"I thought you would be more disturbed by this. Afraid of it."

"Eh," I shrug. "This is the easiest way of solving everybody's problems. Lives get saved, yadda yadda. Happy outcomes. Let's do this. Make the call. Break out your flip phone, buddy. We'll do this."

6

We wait for Rage in the moonlit shadow of Order's web. It's getting cold out. The holiday season is starting to edge its way toward us in a tentative sort of way. I forget about that, because I never participate anymore. Christmas is one of those things that just sort of happens around me, like Valentine's Day, and Halloween, and every other mass vacation event. I sit at the edges of it all, somewhat aware of it because I have to be, but not at all engaged with it.

"I should have brought a warmer jacket," I say. "Didn't expect to be out here so long. Thought I might have some chance at getting home before midnight."

"What home?" He snorts the question with a particular kind of derision.

"What do you mean?"

"I followed your scent. You have no home. You have a room."

"Dude. That is not cool. Have you heard of the concept of privacy? You had no right to break into my house! The fuck!"

"I was curious about you."

"Stalkers are curious about people too. Your curiosity doesn't excuse your creepiness. I don't go breaking into your home. I could have come back here during the day and snooped around here, and I didn't. I respected your space. I..."

He's holding one of his hands up almost all the way in my face. It's good that he has four hands, because if he does that gesture to stop me from talking, he's gonna lose one.

"Calm down," he says, uttering the only two words guaranteed to make someone lose their shit. "I had to investigate you."

"And what did you learn, asshole?"

"I learned that apart from your profession, you have no ties to the world. There is no evidence of even a tenuous familial connection. No pictures. Nothing but piles of books, most of which tell tales of things that never happened. You are a fantasist escaping the repeated horrors inflicted upon you by a job that exposes you to the worst of humanity and the utmost suffering. You are a broken little thing, and you deserve to be looked after better than you are."

Well damn. That's what we in the business call a complete character assassination.

"I am not broken," I seethe. "And I do not need to be looked after. Where is your stupid brother? I would rather have my throat ripped out than listen to this nonsense."

"You have no food in your house."

"Oh my god. I live in New York City! There's food on literally every corner. You know what? You're a fucking moth, so how about you tone down the judgement a little there, flappy."

"You have no home."

"My books are my home. Now shut up. You had no right to go to my apartment, and you have even less right to judge me. I'm here helping you even though you have the sexual morals of a flea and the personal boundaries of a sewer rat."

He chuckles. Nothing I say seems to get under his skin, but he's finding his way under mine almost without effort. It's because he went out of his way to get to know me by breaking into my apartment. I should, and do feel violated, but I can admit to myself that there's a very small part of me that is somewhat flattered this monstrous creature has any interest in me at all. If he was more like his brother, I'd just be dead. Instead, here I am, arguing with him at the top of his lungs while he appears to enjoy the argument.

I suppose I have to give him some cultural leeway. He was hatched, he said. Probably didn't have a mother to tell him not to snoop on people. Probably didn't have anybody to guide him. I wonder if his fellow insect people were responsible for him, or if there's still a mad scientist from the 1940's drinking youth juice and remaining impervious to the effects of time.

I wish I could see where he came from. I intend to get back at him. I intend to find out all about him, just as he seems to have found out all about me.

The beating of wings shuts me up. Acting swiftly, Justice grabs me by the back of the neck and hauls me back against his body, wrapping his lower limbs around my waist. It's a possessive grip, and it reminds me immediately of our wicked embrace yesterday. I feel him stiffen against me immediately, flooding me with the memories of his massive cock. He is built like a monster, and I still ache because of him. There's not enough time for him to fuck me again. I'm slightly disappointed. Being with this moth creature lowers my inhibitions, because nothing seems entirely real.

Rage is here.

I hear a slight jingle as he lands heavily. He still has the cuffs on, apparently unable to free himself of his own accord. It's satisfying to know that he's been suffering a little. If I have my way, he will suffer a lot more. He will serve a sentence commensurate with his crimes.

Rage is slightly smaller than Justice. I wonder if he is younger. Very probably. He has the air of recklessness of youth about him.

"Give me the key," he says, not bothering with so much as a hello. "Actually, give me all of it. I'm going to rip her fucking head off."

"Easy, Rage," Justice says.

"Oh, I get it. You're attached to her. You're such a twisted, perverse fuck," Rage laughs. "You might want to fuck her one last time, because I am going to open her up and feast on her entrails. I owe this human more pain than any of the other humans who came before her."

"She's going to give you the key," he says. "Just hold on a second."

"What do you mean, hold on a second? You called me and told me you had the bitch here and I could do with her what I wanted. Now you're telling me to hold on? Give her here!" He reaches for me with a swipe of claws. His hands are all still cuffed, but he still manages to use them by beating his wings and twisting his body in such a way as to slash across my body.

Claws! Were they there before? I don't know for sure. I do know that I see them clearly now in the night and that they seem sharp enough to slice me from neck to navel. I gasp in a breath, images of his previous victims racing through my mind. I could be hurt here. Badly. I could be gutted and disemboweled before Justice even realizes it. He's holding onto me, but that doesn't give either one of us anything in the way of maneuverability.

"Easy!" Justice booms the order that is not a proper order and hauls me back a step or two. By this stage I have started to struggle for real, my fear palpable now as I attempt to free myself from Justice's grip. I will not simply sit here and let myself get hurt. Fuck no.

"Let me go! Let me fucking go!"

Rage laughs. He's forgotten about his suspicions. My distress has him entirely focused on me now, predator that he is. He makes another one of those bold, aggressive, awkward swipes with his cuffed hands. This time he catches my coat, turning the button up area into a fresh set of fabric ribbons in an instant.

"The fuck!"

Cursing is starting to feel completely pointless, and yet it keeps emerging from me. I cannot help it. Everything about this situation is fucked, including the fact that Justice is not letting me go. He keeps me dangling like the worm on a hook I am, baiting his brother along for some as yet to be determined purpose.

"Justice! Let me go!"

His arms tighten around me, and when the next slash comes for my guts, I sustain a light scratch across the actual bared skin of my belly. A fraction of an inch deeper, and he'll be in the fat layer. A fraction more, and my insides are going to be outside.

Just as I am almost certain that I am going to die from a botched monster sting, Order launches himself from the top of the shipping containers. I didn't see him up there. He must have climbed up in the dark and been waiting for the right moment.

I watch, amazed, as he comes sailing down from that vantage point, webs emerging from his fingers in a splay of material that goes absolutely fucking everywhere.

He lands on Rage, tackling him to the ground, doing his best to coat the angry monster in his sticky web. But Rage is not going to go down that easy. He fights back with his cuffed hands, doing more damage to the webbing and potentially, to Order himself. The spider is agile, used to capturing struggling prey, and Rage is somewhat hobbled by his cuffs, though not as much as I am in Justice's arms.

It's a struggle for him to hold onto me, because I am also trying to break free. The detective and the criminal are both stuck in a battle for what feels like our lives.

"Help me!" Order calls out to Justice. It would seem there are limits to his silk reserves, with Rage cutting through them as quickly as they go on, beating his wings furiously with a rattling, hissing, growling sound. The ambiance is evocative of the very end of the world.

Justice needs to drop me and help Order, or else Rage is about to escape. But Justice doesn't. He just keeps holding onto me, and within the next thirty seconds, Rage gets his wings free and takes to the skies, fleeing with loud cursing.

Order turns to Justice, panting and furious, his sharp teeth exposed with panting breaths. I let out a shriek. His sunglasses have been knocked off his face, and now eight bright blue human eyes blink at us. He has two normal size eyes, another two stacked above them, and then four more that go around the sides of his head at a slightly smaller scale. The effect is nothing short of absolutely fucking terrifying, and it is not helped by the mood he is in, which is furious.

"We lost him because you won't put down your human cuddle toy."

Finally, when it no longer really matters, Justice relinquishes me. I scramble away from the pair of them and make a run not for freedom, but to the gap in the storage containers. I squeeze through that as fast as possible and find myself facing one open door.

"Tessie!"

"Sally!"

"Don't call me that!"

I run into the container and find Tessie wrapped up in web, suspended from both the ceiling and the floor. I wonder if Order would have had enough web to catch Rage if he hadn't already blown his spider load on her. She seems otherwise unharmed, just sort of hanging there with her head exposed and most of her body encased.

"Are you okay?"

"Yeah," she says. "This is more comfy than it looks."

Obigor is sleeping on a pillow nearby. He seems unperturbed, but he is both deaf and exhausted, so he doesn't care.

I look around. This shipping container is not a filthy old empty space. This is an outfitted home with high end but outdated furniture. The style is retro, not quite teal blue with a lot of leathery beige accents that make the space masculine without being aggressive about it. Tall arm chairs are set around a CRT television set resplendent in wooden paneling. The rug beneath my feet has to be handwoven. It is that same blue with white accents of large insect motifs. I have the feeling that I have stepped into a single chamber of what is a very large and expansive above ground burrow that runs back quite deep and branches off all over the place.

"The shipping container was developed later than we were by almost a decade, but when it was, our creator realized it provided the perfect cover. We could be present in plain sight almost anywhere. All we needed was some industrial use space and a few cranes operated by humans who did not know precisely what they were transporting."

I turn around again to see Justice standing in front of me. I do not give a flying moth fuck about the history of shipping containers right now. I have a bigger bone to pick with him.

"You almost let him kill me!"

Justice has the gall to look confused.

"I did tell you that you were going to be bait. You begged to be bait. You do know what happens to bait, correct?"

"He almost got me!"

"Almost," Justice agrees. "But that's just a scratch."

I narrow my eyes. His indifference is unacceptable, both professionally and personally. I know better than to think someone I hooked up with mid-air is going to be the love of my life, but he could at least try to keep me slightly safe.

"You really don't care if you get me, or Tessie, or Obigor killed, do you? It's all about getting what you want, using us as tools, and then leaving when it's all over."

"It had to feel real, Sally."

I gasp and draw back a foot before lunging forward again, my finger pointed against his chest. "Don't you ever use that name audibly. Or inaudibly," I say.

Tessie is laughing, which really pisses me off. I pretend as much as I can not to have a first name. Sally is just so... so many things I do not want to identify with. Old-fashioned, feminine, delicate, wholesome. I wish I had been called something with more edge. Sally is the sort of name that makes a girl desperate to prove herself. Maybe it made me tougher than I'd otherwise be. Whatever. I don't want to hear it coming out of this guy's mouth.

"You have to stay here until morning," he says, changing the subject, or more likely, ignoring me. "Rage has your scent, and he will come back for you. Nowhere will be safe for you tonight besides this place."

He has the whole night to hunt for me, and he's pissed. He's going to be limited with his hands still cuffed together, but he has already proven he's plenty dangerous that way.

"If he goes to my apartment and hurts my books..."

Justice looks very confused. "What do you care about books when your life is at stake?"

"What do you care about my life when you were dangling me like a fucking..."

"You weren't harmed," he growls. "You have a scratch."

"A scratch that's probably infested with mutated bacteria from the claws of someone who uses them to murder people."

"Aww! You two are cute! You know, I always wondered what kind of guy you could possibly end up in a relation-ship with, and a mutated moth monster man is not what I thought of, but it makes sense."

Damn Tessie and her incredible unbothered-ness in this moment.

"I will clean the wound," he says. "Because you are a baby."

"Fuck you, buddy!"

He laughs. He was joking. He has kind of a twisted sense of humor. I wonder how many other jokes of his I missed.

"Come to my room," he says. "I have antiseptic and bandaging."

I want to see his room. He saw my private sanctum sanctorum, it is only fair that I should get to intrude upon his, though it doesn't have quite the same vibe when you're invited.

I leave Tessie dangling, apparently unconcerned by her predicament. I don't know what exactly is going on there, but I do know we are going to have a lot to talk about when this is over.

"Uh."

The next room, Justice's room, is empty. It has a bedroll, the kind that soldiers use on training exercises, and a med kit. Literally nothing else. Fortunately for me, I need what's in the med kit.

"You talked about how weird my place was, and this is yours?"

"This is a room I use to sleep," he says. "The rest of the place accommodates any other needs I have. I don't need anything else in here."

"That's my exact philosophy. I think you were projecting your weirdness onto me. Is that what you need? You need me to be weird like you?"

"Maybe I do," he says gruffly.

Just like that, the mood shifts. There's suddenly something intimate in the air, a release of pheromones, maybe. Or maybe it's just the chemistry of the argument. Whatever it is, some kind of heat is charging between us. I don't trust it.

He turns to me and holds me.

"Stay still," he says. "I need to get all this scary mutant bacteria out of your little boo boo."

"Oh my god, you fucking jerk," I laugh.

He draws me close and hitches me up his body so we can be properly eye to eye. I used to find his red gaze strange. Now it's just kind of hot.

"I missed you," he breathes against my mouth.

"Since yesterday?"

"I could not think of anything other than you. Even Rage occupied less of my mind than he should. You are a distraction. And I do not wish to remain distracted."

"You're hoping to fuck me out of your system? That it?"

It's not typical for men to be this blunt about their desire to use my body to moderate their own emotional state. Usually men at least pretend to want something deeper. They talk about things like love and marriage, they dog whistle about family and kids. They think that's what I want to hear, and so they lie to me ineffectively.

"I want to wrap you around my cock until I fill you with my seed. Your pussy takes my cock like it was made for me. The way you gripped me, how you cried out and took me even though it stretched your cunt so tightly, it was glorious. I don't think there is any way to fuck you out of my system. But I have to have you now."

He knows how to talk his way into my pants, that's for damn sure. I have never been with a creature with so much intense desire for me, at least not one with whom I share the same level of attention.

I can't work out what he wants from me, if he wants anything at all. Right now all he needs is my body and he is going to take it. Two pairs of arms wrap around me and draw me down to that pathetic excuse for a bed. At least I have a mattress at my place, not a thin polystyrene mat on top of a canvas stretcher.

It doesn't really matter though, not really. When I am in his arms it doesn't matter where I am, or what is around us. He has a way of becoming the world. His bright red eyes fill my field of vision, and his agile, plentiful hands work at my clothing almost without me noticing. I don't want to be clothed. I want to be naked. I want to become as he is, an animal, a creature of strangeness and instinct.

When he has stripped me bare, his mouth opens and that wicked, monstrous tongue unfurls around me, wraps about me, finds the little erogenous zones on my neck, right beneath my ear, and then flicks away to tease at the under-side of my nipple, then once again down my stomach to brush ever so lightly against my clit. He is playing my body with his tongue, tasting me, teasing me. The feeling is powerful and yet soft.

He makes me come three times before he pushes that monster cock inside me, slowly this time, drawing out the act of penetration, making me feel every strange inch. I lie beneath him, submissive to his dominant desire, absolutely wrapped up in my own sexual need.

Justice is fucking good in bed. He knows when to go slow and when to go hard. He knows how to make a soft little flick of his tongue against my clit so I can take another inch of that fucking huge cock. I am whimpering to myself, feeling that borderline sensation between pleasure and pain. Being with him hurts, but it hurts good.

"You're mine," he says, stopping with his cock deep inside me. "This mating means something to me. It is my claim over you. I have drunk the nectar of your need. I have filled you with my seed. You are not a passing fancy. I want you as my mate."

"I..." I don't get a chance to respond because he has started to thrust, and every surging stroke of his cock deep inside me chases the thoughts and linguistic capabilities that once accompanied them right out of my head. He is fucking my brains out, using that tongue of his not only to tease my clit, but soaking it in the juices between us. He makes me so fucking wet, something he seems to be doing by design.

He pulls his cock free and turns me over, all four hands gripping me firmly as he lifts my ass up toward him and he proceeds to lick and drink my arousal from the lips of my pussy. I am like a sexual flower to him, a source of sustenance.

"I never know whether to spank you, fuck you, or feed on you," he purrs against my sex. His tongue has coiled up inside his mouth again and his lips are on my pussy. He uses the coil inside me, penetrating my body, soaking himself in my juices.

"Just fuck me. I'm a good girl," I moan, desperate for that thick cock to return once more.

"You are no such thing," he says, slapping my ass. "You make me want to thrash you every time I talk to you, with your sass and your arrogance. You deserve to be put over my knee and spanked long and hard, but I cannot resist this..."

He lowers me back down to his cock and thrusts it up inside me, filling my dripping sex in one dominant thrust. "This cunt of mine," he growls in my ear. "This tight human hole that I have claimed for my own. You will give it to me when I desire it. You will bare your flesh for me, and I will use you as I see fit."

Every one of those words is accompanied by a slow, pumping thrust. One of his hands has moved around to cup my pussy from the front. He holds me there and has me grind my clit against his powerful hand as his cock stretches me over and over.

Justice's lovemaking is powerful and dominant. He makes no apologies for it. He makes me feel soft and tender and cared for in the most carnal of ways. He wants me to come. He spanks my pussy lightly, dick deep inside me.

"Show me another one of those pretty little orgasms," he growls, tapping my pussy and my clit at the same time. "Don't make me spank this sweet little cunt too hard. You don't want to be too sore, do you?"

I am arched against him, my cunt gripping his cock as he spank-fucks me to a twisted orgasm, firm fingers rubbing and slapping my pussy until I start to gasp and squeal from the sensation. Orgasms, plural, are rolling through me, but one, two, three, they are not enough. He spanks my pussy like I am his naughty girl who deserve to have her pussy punished and filled.

"Fuck," he growls, uttering a rare curse as my inner walls grip him tighter and tighter, and finally he cannot resist the call of my writhing cunt on his cock. He pulls me down firmly on his dick and comes inside me in hard thrusting spurts.

He pulls free from me and lets it spill from me, my stretched pussy relinquishing all that cum in a hot flow over my aching, stinging, sore sex.

"This is going to hurt in the morning," I mumble.

"Good," he purrs back. "I like you sore and submissive."

I'd tell him to fuck off, but I'm too sleepy, at least at first.

Sometime in the middle of the night, I find myself lying in his arms on his bed roll, feeling like a terrible detective. Somewhere out there, a furiously betrayed murderer is once more preying on the world at large, and I am hiding in bed with a man — or something close enough to a man — because I want pleasure and safety. When the hell did I start to want either of those things?

We've left Rage to rampage through the city unchecked. I have to hope that he has not done any damage to an innocent citizen.

"What are you doing?" He reaches around my hip and cups my pussy, as if reminding me there will be pain if I give him trouble.

"What now? The FBI will be taking over the case any day now, and..."

"Stop," he says, his voice deep and resonant.

"Stop?"

"It doesn't matter what happens out there. We are trying, but we cannot do what cannot be done."

That feels like a tautology, but okay.

"I need to keep you safe," he says simply, patting my aching pussy. "The rest of the city can take care of itself for one night. Get some rest. You're exhausted."

He is not wrong. The adrenaline from being used as bait has metabolized into other things, pleasure among them. I have had orgasms ripped from me in healing tsunamis. Now I want nothing more than to lie my head against the powerful thorax of the mothman who has claimed me, close my eyes, and get some sleep.

7

Tessie and I are in the office, hungover the way you are when you've been through some shit. Even Obigor has more of a thousand-yard cataract stare than usual.

We drove back from the shipping container complex in silence, both staring ahead of ourselves at the road, saying nothing. What do you say to your partner when you accidentally signed her up for a night of suspension bondage? I tried saying sorry, but she just sort of brushed me off before I could ask any real questions.

We've retreated to our office which now provides us with some insulation from everything going on in the station. There was a buzz when we came in, so we avoided eye contact, spoke to no one, and made a bee-line for our desks.

Now we're attempting to make ourselves presentable. Tessie has a bit of webbing in her hair. I almost reach out to take it off her, but then I remember how sticky that shit is. Last thing I need is to end up stuck to her head.

"You've got spider cum in your hair," I tell her.

"Wha?" She blushes. "No, I don't. What are you... no!"

"The web shit. It's in your hair."

"Oh," she says. "Oh, fuck."

At that moment, the chief bangs on the door in the closed fist way some men do because they forget that glass, and basically everything is more fragile than they are. He throws the door open and gives us a look I don't like. It's not his usual grump. It's something that makes him less angry, more sad.

"Officer Peterson from the 96th was murdered last night," he says bluntly. "Same MO as your perpetrator. Nothing was taken but his keys."

I have never felt the intensity of crushing guilt that I do in this moment. An officer is dead. This is my fault. Instead of chasing Rage down, we let him go. He found a way to get his cuffs off.

"I am so sorry, sir."

"Don't be sorry. Find the asshole."

"Yes. Sir."

He shuts the door. That's it.

I am furious. Furious at myself, but almost equally as angry with Justice. We curled up and slept while a brave man was slaughtered. One of our own.

Tessie looks at me, wide-eyed. "We should have done something."

"Yes. We should have. And we're going to."

I get up and stride toward the door. I hear Tessie say something, but I'm not listening. Blood is rushing in my ears. I know exactly what I'm going to do.

I am going to kill Rage.

It's the only way to ensure that he doesn't end up in the justice system and reveal Justice's secret to the world. It also ensures nobody else dies. This is the sort of thing we are very much trained not to do. We are not supposed to take the law into our own hands. But I do not see what other choice I have. Rage is happy to murder and destroy, and Justice seems unable to reason with him, let alone contain him. That webbing was nothing, or maybe there wasn't enough. I don't know. What I do know is that there's one bug about to get swatted.

I have several hours of daylight and a pretty fucking good idea where he is. The body of Officer Peterson was found not far from a Red Light Discount store. There's a chance Rage changed his habits after I caught him the first time, but given how badly that went for me, I doubt he feels actually compelled to make any adjustments. He thinks he's untouchable, and that is precisely the arrogance that is going to let me take him out.

I tell myself it's not really murder, what I'm about to do. It's more like extermination. Nope. That doesn't make it feel any better. Feels worse. Feels bad because I know what I am about to do is wrong, against everything I stand for, and against the moral of the law I signed up for, if not precisely the letter of that law. Nobody says you can't kill monsters. You're supposed to slay them.

I reach the store without too much trouble, mostly because I took Tessie's car. Huh. Didn't even notice I'd done that. Oh well.

I get out of the car and head right to the inevitable alley. Brooklyn loves itself an alley. It's like hives of scum and villainy built right into almost every block. Rage is surrounded by filth, addicts, criminals. He blends in with all of them, but I see him. I know the shape of him. That dangerous V pressed against the alley wall, those two antennae twitching ever so slightly with the breeze.

I'm plainclothes, as usual. Nobody has any reason to suspect I'm here to take a life, but I feel as though I'm giving out a very specific energy, one that makes most of the inhabitants of the alley scatter out of it.

I walk slowly toward the sleeping monster. I wonder what he's dreaming of. Perhaps disemboweling another officer of the law, or perhaps a father of two. The heinous thoughts of a creature like him cannot be fathomed. I suppose now I am learning what it is like to be on the verge of taking life, to savor that moment of complete power over another being, to know that by my action, I will end one complete universe. Something unique is before me, and I will end it because it is evil.

Standing behind him, I lift my weapon. It is best I do this quickly, before someone sees a woman in an alley pointing a gun at a bit of wall. There is life all around us, busyness that will not allow anyone to notice what is happening here.

I push the gun against his head. I thought it would be easier to pull the trigger. *Just pull the fucking trigger.* But I don't.

Or I can't. I don't know why. He deserves to die. He has to die.

He's helpless. That's the fucking problem. It doesn't feel sporting to just walk up and shoot someone who isn't expecting it, even a cop-killing monster.

"Hey, asshole," I say. That's enough warning.

He laughs at me, swings around, and grabs at me with all four of his hands. I lost the split-second advantage of surprise and now I am just as helpless as the rest of his victims.

The junkies scatter as the alley erupts into violence. Nobody here is laying down their lives for anybody else. They're saving their own skin, and it's a good move.

Rage pulls me into the dumpster. Foul smells and worse substances coat us both as he attempts to choke the life out of me. His MO is to slash at his victim's belly and rend them open. He tries to do just that. His claws hit the kevlar of my bulletproof vest. I did not come unprepared.

"Weren't expecting that, were you motherfucker?"

This is now self-defense.

I shoot him. I pull the trigger at point blank range, and all the parts of him capable of entertaining a thought or planning a murder become grime, fluid, and biomass. The sound damn near makes my ear drums rupture, but there's no time to worry about hearing loss. I need to get out of this filthy tomb before I throw up.

It takes seconds for me to throw myself out of the dumpster. I pull my turtleneck off, wipe my bloodied face off, and toss it back in the dumpster.

Retreating to the car, I make a call.

"Hey, Hank. Can I get a pick up on a dumpster? Yeah. Brooklyn. Alley between Forsyth and Hencher. Gonna need that done ASAP, bud. Drop at the usual place."

Hank is a man who could be in prison, but is not, and that is all anybody needs to know about him.

It takes twenty minutes, but Hank shows up. He backs his truck down the alley like a pro and hooks that dumpster up like it's his business. I suppose it is.

Hank is thickset, with heavy brows, dark hair, and an abundance of body hair. He wears oil-stained blue overalls that bring out his bright blue eyes. He must have been very handsome when he was young, in a Brando sort of way. Middle age has transformed him, as it no doubt will transform us all. He's still handsome, but in a more accessible sort of way.

He gives me a slight wave as he pulls out, taking the evidence of my crime away with him. The dumpster is on its way to a place where a lot of criminals drop a lot of things. *Criminals.* The word sticks in my mind. Am I one of them now? My hands are shaking slightly. When I look down at them, I see there's a fine mist that used to be Rage.

Next thing I know, I'm in the shower. Not entirely sure how I got here, but I have to assume it was in the ordinary way. My brain isn't tracking as it usually does.

My phone is ringing. I step out of the shower to answer it, not bothering to turn the shower off or put a towel on. I just drip where I stand, butt naked.

"Hello?"

"Where the hell are you?"

"Just having a shower?"

"You took my car ten hours ago. Obigor and I need to go home."

"Shit. Did I? Fuck. Sorry. I'll bring it back to the station now."

"What have you..."

I disconnect the call. I have got to get my shit together. I cannot afford to fall apart now.

When I glance out the window, I notice that night is starting to fall. Have I been showering for hours? My skin does seem particularly pink in spots, and sensitive. You could even say raw, especially on the backs of my hands when I was covered in parts of a recently departed sentient creature. I should probably get some moisturizer on those.

"Where have you been!?" Tessie is not pleased to see me. Obigor isn't either, but he greets me anyway in case I have any secret flavors on my skin. He licks my hand with his little tongue. I yank my hand away with a hiss. It feels like sandpaper being dragged over a raw wound.

"What the..." Tessie gets up, hops to the door, and shuts it, pulling the blinds down with quick snapping motions. "What have you done?"

"Uh. Nothing."

"You look like you just saw a ghost," she says. "Or made one."

Sometimes I forget Tessie is a detective in her own right. She may not do much in the way of fieldwork, but she has interrogated more people than I can count. Thousands, probably. She knows what guilt looks like.

"Do you really want me to tell you?"

She sits down and pulls open her snack drawer. This is a drawer I am supposed to pretend does not exist. It is her private stash. She feels the same way about this drawer as I do about my apartment. She grabs the most chocolatey of bars and hands it to me. "Eat this," she says. "Before you pass the fuck out."

I thought my hands were shaking from all of the murder. Maybe I'm not so much racked by guilt as suffering from low blood sugar. I take a bite and immediately feel nauseous.

"I'm good," I say, wrapping the wrapper carefully over the end, hiding the nub of my nibble.

"You are absolutely not good," she says. "You're pale, sweaty, and you can't eat. Either you're coming down with one hell of a flu, or you did something you wish you hadn't."

"I had to do it. I wish it hadn't been so gross."

Tessie doesn't react. She's using her interrogation skills on me. I could say anything now and she wouldn't show any sign of horror or similar emotion. She's just going to listen and build the case against me, let me hang myself with my own rope.

"You know you're not in trouble, right?" she says. "I mean, he wasn't a person. There are no laws against killing an animal, which for all intents and purposes, that's what he was."

"Was he?"

"I mean, lawyers will argue it back and forth, but he wasn't a person."

He was a person to Justice, though. He was a brother. He was someone Justice was trying to protect. It's not human law I am worried about. It's natural law. Specifically, Order and Justice.

"I'm taking you to my place tonight," she says. "I don't like the way you look, and I don't think hanging out at the station is going to be any good for you, either."

"Okay."

Usually I'd argue, but I don't feel like arguing right now. I feel like being somewhere I don't have to be myself, because what myself did today has probably shattered anything that might ever have happened between Justice and me. I have betrayed Justice. I can pretend I didn't, but I did.

"Let's go."

I'm at Tessie's apartment. She also has a small place, but hers is more traditionally appointed. It has a functioning kitchen, for starters. She's making something in it while I stare at my phone. I'm not looking at anything in particular. I'm just looking in general.

"He's going to hate me."

"Who?" She frowns. "Chief's going to love you. He might not ever really know why, but he will be glad a murderer is off the street."

"Justice."

"Oh. The moth. Yeah. He might not be a fan. I think you should lay low for a while. Take some leave. You're not okay, Sally."

"Yeah, I guess so."

"See. That's how bad you are. I just called you Sally and you didn't even freak out on me."

Huh. Guess I didn't.

8

I'm in a state of something like shock for about a week before I start to feel myself again, before the oddness and the guilt begin to be absorbed by everyday life. Obviously, the murders stop. There aren't too many questions asked. The proximity of the death of Officer Peterson to the end of the serial killer's reign of terror is not thought to be of any significance.

Officially, the murders remain open cases. Unofficially, everybody knows that one of us took matters into their own hands and nobody is going to say a fucking thing about it. The Chief gives me a nod and a smile on my way into work most days now, which is about as explicit a sign as possible that he knows.

After seven days of something like mourning, but more like freaking out, I decide it's time to get back to normal. I can't stay at Tessie's forever. I have to reclaim my life.

It feels good to be back among my things, surrounded by my stories. Even if I don't open the books, they feel like armor.

It is a pleasure unlike any other to take one of them and crawl into bed, losing myself in the troubles of another person who will be scared and then brave and then lose and then win.

Engrossed in a story, I've almost forgotten about my heinous actions when a sudden pounding at my front door makes me jump. It's not the sound of knocking. It's the sound of the latch being forced open. In an instant, I am regretting ever having come back here. I should have moved. I should have left the fucking city.

I find myself breathing very shallowly and pressing hard up against the mattress, trying to flatten myself as the door clicks open, and a tall figure stoops under the frame.

Motherfucker. I forgot Justice had broken in here before. I stay still. I guess at this point, I'm going to have to pretend I am asleep. Hopefully he spontaneously develops some awareness of how rude he is being and leaves.

Nope.

"There you are!" Justice exclaims loudly, as if he has some kind of right to wake me the fuck up in my own apartment. I'm glad he's being an asshole. That's going to make this easier for both of us.

I open my eyes. He is standing over me, bright red eyes flaring with emotion, shirtless torso and all four arms rippling with irritated muscularity. In my guilt, I had forgotten how hot he was.

"I have been looking for you everywhere! I thought you were dead! Do you have any idea how worried I've been?"

I'm only just hearing the lecture through an absolute whirl-wind of shame.

"I can take care of myself," I tell him. "I don't need you hovering about, breaking into my apartment."

"What?" He seems confused. "You left my place a week ago, and I haven't seen you since. I also haven't seen Rage. What happened?"

Shit. He's put two and two together.

I get up out of bed and walk to my front door. He follows me out into the hall, at which point I dart back inside and close the door on him.

Two big hands wrap around the edge of the door and stop it from closing. He pushes his way into my apartment, stooping under the door frame to allow his big head and antennae to get in.

"What is going on with you?"

"Uh, my dude, we are strangers to one another. We might have had sex a couple of times, but you don't know me, so don't act like you do."

He scowls. "Before I beat you, I'm going to give you one last chance to explain what this attitude is about. Something has happened. I thought it had happened to you. I'm very glad it hasn't. I thought Rage had found you."

"Beat me? No, man. We're done. Trust me. We are done."

"Trust me, we are not," he growls. "There's something between us. I missed you. Are you telling me you didn't miss me?"

"Did I come find you?"

I hate being a bitch, but being a bitch is going to make this easier. Maybe. I don't know. I know that the impulse I am having to throw myself into his arms and beg for his forgiveness has to be resisted at all costs. I don't deserve his kindness or his care. I've got to get rid of him. Now.

"Get the fuck outta here," I say.

"No," he replies. "There is something wrong with you."

"Really, the freak with the wings and the antennae thinks there's something wrong with me?"

That was cruel. He'll leave now, for sure.

But he doesn't. He picks me up with all four hands and carries me back to my bed.

"You and I don't really know one another completely yet," he says. "But I know enough about you to tell when you're lying, and every word out of your mouth right now is some kind of lie."

"I'm not going to have sex with you."

"No," he says. "You're not. You're going to have your underwear taken down and your bottom spanked until you tell me what's happening."

He makes good on that threat, sitting down on my bed and sweeping me over his powerful thigh. My pajamas give up the fight without issue, retreating down to my knees with a sweep of his hand.

He has three hands to hold me down with, in addition to the one that will punish me. One holds me by the back of the head. Another pins my right arm to the center of my back. The third snugs my hip against his stomach, and the fourth comes down across my ass in a hard slap that makes me scream. It's not that he's hit me terribly hard, it's that the shock of the slap unleashes everything I've been holding in.

From that first slap, I wail. He doesn't stop. If he is concerned at the oddity of the intensity of my reaction, he doesn't show it. He just keeps me where he wants me and paints my ass with a fraction of the pain I deserve. I don't fight. I don't struggle. There's no point anyway. If he doesn't want to let me go, then he is not going to let me go. I am here for as long as he decides I should be.

I start to sob as the heat flashes through me, big, hot tears running down my cheeks. Still he spanks me with those stern slaps that catch the lower part of my cheeks, right where I would sit. This is the kind of spanking that has no erotic heat. This is the kind of spanking that is just designed to punish a bad girl who deserves it.

I know I deserve it. I find myself arching my hips up so every time his big palm lands it catches even more of my bare, naked skin. This might be the last time he touches me, ever.

"I told you that you were mine," he says. "Did you not understand what that meant? It means you don't run from me, you don't hide from me, and you absolutely do not disappear for a week and let me think you are dead."

A flurry of hot, harsh slaps punctuate that sentence, driving a crescendo of heat, shame and soreness that takes my sobbing tears and turns them into absolute howls of contrition.

He stops. He sits me up on his lap, and he brushes stray hair out of my face so that his ruby red gaze can bore into mine with a piercing expression that makes me almost certain he knows already.

"Shhh," he soothes me, even as my ass feels like molten lava trapped beneath tight skin. "Shh, it's okay. I still love you. You're okay. You were in trouble, but you're okay."

"Not okay!" I sob out, struggling to get myself under control. He has broken down all my reserves and left me at the mercy of my emotions. How am I supposed to keep lying to us both like this?

"This isn't like you," he says. "You fight everything tooth and nail. Something happened," he says. "Tell me what."

His voice is low and comforting. He uses one of his thumbs to brush tears from my cheek and waits, patiently. I feel my mouth open. I feel words start to form. I don't feel like I am in control of them, or of myself. When I pulled the trigger, I did something irredeemable. What happens next is inevitable.

"No," I say, surprising myself with my ability to keep my secret even when I don't think I can anymore. "I can't tell you. It's too bad."

He shifts slightly, resettling me on his lap. The small motion reignites the heat in my ass, reminding me of his dominance and soon to be disappointment. "Whatever it is, it cannot be that bad."

But it is that bad. I'd rather push him away than have him discover what I did and hate me. That's probably selfish.

No, not probably, definitely. I should tell him, and then he'd know. He could move on with his life.

"Sally," he says, using my name. Usually that word ignites a response of disgust and rebellion from me. This time it makes me start weeping as the confession tumbles out of me of its own accord.

"I killed him."

"What?"

"He killed a police officer. I found him a second time, and he got hold of me, so I shot him." It sounds blunt when I say it that way, but blunt is the only way to confess. I've seen criminals explain things this way before, with the same level of apparent detachment. It never occurred to me their stomachs might be swirling with guilt. It's absolutely fucked up how different the inside and outside of a person can be at the same time.

"Alright, so hate me now, or revenge kill me, whatever," I say.

There is a long pause. The worst possible of all things: silence.

Is he going to kill me for revenge? Am I going to be another mutilated moth victim? I brace myself for the end I am sure I probably deserve.

"I'm sorry," he says softly.

I close my eyes, thinking he's apologizing for what he is about to do to me.

"Just make it quick," I mumble. "I did that for him."

"Christ," Justice swears. "I'm not going to kill you. What kind of monster do you think I am?"

I open my eyes and look into his monstrous face, his eyes, his antennae, the all-too-human nose and mouth, hard jaw, the handsomeness and the monstrousness blended together in a predatory chimera.

"The kind to avenge a fallen brother?"

That's the kind of monster I am. That's what I did. Without thinking.

He draws in a deep breath and lets out a sad sigh. "I said I am sorry because I should have killed him myself. Instead, I let the job fall to you. You did what had to be done, and you did it at the expense of your moral code and, I suspect, your sanity. That burden should never have fallen on your shoulders. I know you were under pressure to catch the responsible party. I knew that human lives were at stake. I failed you. You did nothing wrong."

"You're not angry with me?"

"No. I wanted to have everything, and I should have known that I could not have everything. I wanted to capture Rage, protect lives, and have you. Those three things weren't all possible. In the end, you made the decision."

He is stroking my hair and holding me close, comforting me. This is the most surprising interaction of all. Far more surprising than discovering that mothmen are real. I have never had a partner like this, who respected my strength, took responsibility for his own failings, who refused to let my walls stand, but made himself safe for me when they fell.

I feel the most overwhelming welling of love from him and for him. I feel cared for and cherished. I feel a whole host of emotions, some of which I've never experienced in my life.

Tears start to roll down my cheeks, but they're no longer tears of guilt and fear. Instead, they are tears of relief. He understands me, and that understanding feels like the greatest gift I have ever received.

Justice holds me through all of them, rocking me a little until my eyes dry themselves.

"I can't believe you'd forgive me for that."

"I haven't forgiven you, because there's nothing to forgive," Justice says simply. "Rage chose his path. We tried to intervene, and he chose further violence. It's tragic, but I cannot pretend that he or I have been wronged."

"That's very logical for someone who just lost his brother."

"I was hatched with dozens of others," Justice explains. "I am closer to some than others. I wanted to save his life if it was possible, but he was too far gone. I would rather have you breathing than him."

Blunt, but fair.

"I just have one question," he says, his tone heavy.

"Ask it."

"Where is the body?"

"Oh! Uhm." I hadn't actually thought about the logistics of all that would follow confession. "I can show you. It's safe."

"Good. I would like to take him home. Give him a proper burial."

A proper burial is a good idea, and it will ensure that nobody stumbles across a disfigured but undeniably monstrous corpse. If anybody were to find Rage's body, shit would certainly hit the fan.

Now that I am no longer absolutely frozen with fear at the prospect of Justice discovering my crime, I find myself able to think more clearly. Colors seem brighter. The world is less threatening. Things are going to be okay, maybe.

"I need to make a call," I tell him.

"Okay." He gives me a squeeze. There is nothing like a comforting hug from two sets of arms at once. He holds me very close, for a long time, until I exhale and relax against him. "There is nothing I could not forgive you for," he says. "Some things I may need to punish you for, but you will never be unwanted. Do you understand that?"

"Mmnghh," I answer. My face is pressed against his neck. I don't want to say any more than that. I don't know how to take that kind of a declaration of devotion. I don't feel like I have earned it, and there is a part of me wondering if this is actually real, or if it is like it is when we are wanting to recover a body from a murderer. Everybody is friends until the location is confirmed. That's when the Mrs Nice Lady act drops.

If that is what he is doing, there's nothing I can do. I've accepted my fate. Time will tell if Justice truly feels love for me, or if he just wants to recover the body.

He watches and listens to me as I make the call.

"Yeah?"

"Hey. Hank. Do you still have the, uh..."

"Yeah," he says. "I've got it. Had it sitting in the warehouse since you called. Been waiting for instructions."

I completely forgot to get in touch with him. Or maybe it wasn't so much forgetting as it was a refusal to deal with the reality of my actions.

"Alright. Can you load it on a truck. Just a general flatbed. You didn't open the container did you?"

"I don't open nothing I'm not told to open."

I believe him. Hank is a man who has seen enough things that cannot be unseen. He's not going to play peekaboo with a body in a dumpster.

"Alright. See you soon."

"I need to go get, everything," I tell him. "I can meet you at your shipping containers, or..."

"I am not letting you out of my sight," he growls. "Not after the last week, thinking you were forever gone."

Now I feel guilty for a whole other reason. It's like there's no escape from the burden of feeling once you get involved with someone.

"Listen. I thought there was no way you'd ever want to see me again. I thought I'd done something so heinous I was never going to be right with you, or the law, or whatever passes for a god around here again. What I did was wrong. No matter how many people tell me it was reasonable or even a good act, I know it was wrong. I know..."

He grabs me again as my voice starts to crack.

"This is the problem when good girls go bad," he says. "It's not easy feeling outside the law when you're used to being inside it. Those rules don't just protect the public. They make you feel safe too. But now you know you don't always play by those rules. You thought you had a limit, but limits are always moving. I never thought I'd love a normal woman. I never thought I'd encounter anybody as strong as you, as defiant as you, as beautiful as you. But I did, and so my limit changed."

"You are equating me killing Rage to you falling for me."

"In a way," he says.

"It's not the same thing. It's wrong to kill."

He pauses, the corner of his lips twisting wryly before he replies.

"Do you want another spanking? How about a whipping? I can entertain your desire for punishment, Sally. I can put you in a cage of my own making and you can serve your sentence on your knees."

My jaw drops. I'm not sure how to respond to him. I feel my face flushing bright red. He's right, this guilt is making me yearn for punishment. Going over his knee isn't enough to atone for taking life the way I did, in a fit of temper and righteous grief.

"I think you do," he chuckles. "Let's go get this vehicle."

"I trust Hank with a lot of things," I say. "But I don't trust him with seeing you. I should go on my own. Don't worry.

I'll be fine. I can come back here when I'm done, and you can sneak down into the cab."

"Sounds like a plan."

9

I've got a body in a dumpster on the back of my truck, and a mothman tucked up into the bed space of my cab. Everything I need for a wild fucking roadtrip.

"You ready to go?" I ask the question over my shoulder.

"Sure," Justice says.

"I am sorry," I repeat. "I know this is fucked up. He was…"

"An asshole who tried to kill you. Don't worry," Justice says. "My feelings are not as intense as you might imagine. We were taught better than this. He knew what he was doing, and he had to have known what the end might be. Let's go home."

Home. He says it as though it is where we all belong. Wouldn't that be nice.

∼

I t's about a nine-hour drive from New York to West
Virginia. Not that long of a trip, really, except when
you're doing it in a truck. The plan is to start early, around
four in the morning while Justice is still awake enough to
get in the cab, drive through the early morning, and get in
around noon. He'll still be asleep then, but I'll park up at
the address he gave me and wait for him to wake up. When
night falls, he'll show me to what I guess counts as his home.
I'm not sure what will happen then.

I t's about midday in some buttfuck state that's not New
York when a prick with a highway cruiser puts his lights
on and decides to ruin my plans.

"You got a tail light out," the highway patrolman says when
he's done slow-sauntering all the way from his car to my
window. He's tall and skinny and has one of those long
faces.

"I'm sorry, officer," I say. I hand over my badge with my
license and registration, expecting that to be the end of
things. It's not the end of things. He glances over my docu-
ments and hands them back to me, then casts his eye back
over the truck in a manner that suggests he's going to waste
my fucking time.

"New York City Deeeetective," he says, drawing out the
word *detective* almost like it's a bad thing. "Think you're
pretty special, huh?"

"Nope."

"Uh huh." He sucks his teeth and jerks his head back. "What have you got in the dumpster?"

For fuck's sake. I have Justice hiding in the bed area, and Rage's body doing what bodies do in the dumpster. I have no intention of submitting to an inspection right now.

"Garbage, mostly."

His eyes light up, like he's caught me in some kind of lie. "Why are you driving garbage from New York to West Virginia?"

"Police business."

"Uh huh. You got any paperwork? It's not exactly legal to dump garbage across state lines, and I don't have any reason to believe..."

"How about you talk to my boss," I say, dialing my cell phone. I hand it to the cop before the chief answers.

"Yep. Hi. Got one of your so-called detectives out here playing garbage lady. Any paperwork for that, or..."

He doesn't get to finish the sentence. I can hear the chief tearing strips off him from all the way up here in the cab.

"Alright. I think he wants to talk to you," the highway patrolman says, handing the phone back up to me and making a quick exit. Thank god. I was counting on the chief's temper to get the guy off my back, but I know he's not going to be happy with me either.

"Sir, I can explain," I begin to babble.

"Listen. Holmes. There's been a lot of shit going on lately, and I know you've been doing it hard. When you come in on Monday, I don't want to fucking know why you were driving a dumpster to Virginia. We clear?" Chief growls down the line.

"Crystal, sir."

He disconnects the call.

"I am so lucky to work for that man," I say to myself before raising my voice a little. "You alright back there?"

A light snore answers me. Justice fast asleep, trusting me completely. That's quite sweet in a way, considering the full context of this visit, and the fact we were very nearly just busted.

10

"Welcome to the vault," Justice says as the brakes of the truck squeal to a halt in deep forest a long way off what feels like a main road. Night has fallen and our plan has gone off without any more hitches.

I glance around at the signage that meets us. Affixed to a large metal gate are rust-marked warnings from long ago, lit by floodlights. Insects swarm the lights and dance about madly as we come to a halt at the gated perimeter.

There's nothing terribly welcoming to be seen here, though the signs have a great deal more artistic merit to them than modern signage tends to have. The fonts are cheerful and thick, and the military badging is bold and bright, with teal and red accents.

MILITARY PERSONNEL ONLY

KEEP OUT

TRESPASSERS WILL BE EXECUTED.

The last sign is accompanied by line art of a man with crosses for eyes and his tongue lolling out of his mouth dangling from a rope.

"I am experiencing feelings of foreboding," I tell Justice. He smiles, as if my feelings are understandable but unnecessary. I notice that his antennae are both angled forward right now, almost as if eager to return to his home.

"Pull up to the speaker box," he says, gesturing to another anachronistic piece of technology assailed by time. I had assumed there was no way it would function, but it crackles to life when I edge the truck another foot or two forward.

Justice leans over me, which gives me all the excitement of wings in my face.

"Justice returning," he says.

There's no verbal response, but the big imposing gate cranks open, allowing us access to an even more overgrown and imposing road. The gate moves smoothly, suspiciously so. Someone has been maintaining select parts of this compound while deliberately keeping a derelict air.

Every instinct I have is telling me to put this thing into reverse and get the hell out of dodge. We are no longer in the world as I know it. This is like stepping back in time, or maybe out of it completely. Behind these gates, Boomers are still babies. Nothing of the last seventy years has happened. Some would consider this a paradise.

"They'll be waiting for us," Justice says, as I hesitate. It's not precisely what I want to hear or the impetus to get me moving, but curiosity wins out and I put my foot down. Like Jonah and the whale, I am going in.

The road curves this way and that before the foliage parts to reveal what looks like an old factory. Yellow-beige paint no doubt absolutely dripping with lead is peeling from the concrete walls. The entrance is beneath a large semicircular portico ringed with old steel. I can imagine this was once a very impressive facility. Now it is clearly in a state of decay. I can smell rot, or something like it. Something earthy and insect-y, like freshly turned rotting mulch.

"Let's get out," he says. "We're here."

I don't want to get out of the truck. I feel more than a little trepidation. This place is deeply creepy. I have a keen sense of being watched by many, many eyes. Given the creatures who live here, that could mean one or two, or anywhere up to half a dozen cryptid mutants.

I glance over at Justice.

"Why don't you go in and see them, unload the cargo. I'll take the truck back to Hank."

"We didn't just come to deliver Rage," he reminds me. "We're here because I want to show you where I came from."

When he puts it like that, it seems churlish to refuse a home tour. It is the desire not to be rude or insensitive that gets me out of the truck, emotional pressure of the kind I rarely succumb to. I have a weird tingling feeling in my lower stomach. I write that off to nerves, though. I know there are others like Justice here. I am standing on the precipice of something truly secret and odd. This is where creatures of myth and legend were made. This is where the world stopped making sense. The sensation grows. I feel a little nauseous.

Justice reaches out and takes my hand in his lower right hand. His upper right hand settles lightly, but firmly on the back of my neck. I am not sure if his touch is commanding or comforting. It might be both.

I am propelled toward glass doors which have been immaculately cleaned. No fly dirt or spider webs mar the hinges of this entrance. As we enter, the interior of the building reminds me a lot of the interior of his shipping container house, except it is larger.

The 1940's and 50's have been preserved here in complete detail. Nothing has been replaced or upgraded. Everything is as it was. The effect is of walking into an entirely different world, complete with alternative color palette. Teal formica is everywhere, as are rounded corners and smooth metal finishes. We walk into a lobby of sorts, or something like a waiting room. The beige linoleum has been mopped recently, and not a speck of dust has accumulated anywhere, but the place is empty.

"Where is everyone? I thought you said they were waiting for us?"

"Do you really want to meet everyone?"

I'm taken somewhat aback by that question. Of course I want to meet his family. I am nervous as fuck, but I am also curious. I am in the center of a mystery, perhaps even a conspiracy that I've never heard of before. This is the sort of thing a detective dreams of. I became a member of the force to serve and protect, of course, but I also always had an irrepressible urge to ferret the truth out, to know what others didn't know. Mystery has always drawn me, and I am standing in the faintly bleach smelling center of what might be the biggest and best-kept secret of the modern age.

"Of course I do."

"Let me give you an orientation before we do any introductions. I want you to understand some of the details of this place. It will save you from having to ask some of the many questions you will no doubt have, detective."

"Alright."

He leads me to a wall in the lobby where there are black and white portraits of three old men hanging.

"These are Maclyn McCarty, Oswald Avery, and Colin MacLeod. These were the men who discovered the very nature of DNA. Our father was a research assistant in their laboratory, a man of little means, but great ambitions. He wanted not only to create new life, but to save it."

I nod, as Justice seems to expect some kind of response to that.

"That discovery was officially made one year before the end of the Second World War, in 1944, but of course the research had taken place years prior to the public announcement. Our father brought peace to the world through a savant's understanding of this work. He understood more than they ever shared, and the work he did here changed the course of history."

"What was his name? Why are they here but not him?"

"Some people prefer their names be lost to history."

"Why did he make you? And those like you? There's no way you were ever going to fit in with everyday society. Especially not then."

"We were not designed to be freaks. We were designed to be soldiers, with traits common to some insects and other creatures that allow them to withstand some of the cruel chemical conditions humans began to inflict upon one another. Many of our older brothers and sisters were sacrificed to end the conflict."

"I thought atomic weapons were used against civilians to end the war."

"Yes. There were many monstrous undertakings. The atomic bomb could not be hidden from the world. Other secrets were better kept. Like us. To this day, our mission is to protect people. We function as guardians of humanity, as and where we can. What Rage did was a complete perversion of his purpose, not to mention all we were raised to believe in. He was like a sheep dog who turned on his flock. His death was inevitable."

"So your family won't be angry at me for killing him?"

"My family sent me to bring him back in the state he is in. They do not need to know the specifics of what happened. You do not need to take the blame."

"So they won't know why I am here. I'm just your side piece."

"Actually, your presence here has already raised some brows," he says. "No humans besides our fathers have ever been permitted inside these walls."

"So why did you bring me here?"

"Because we need you."

"Uh. Flattering, I guess, but I don't think that's true."

"So this is her?"

We are interrupted by a deep, rough voice. Justice's family has decided to take the introductions into their own hands. I turn and am greeted with what I can only describe as a man-monarch. He is not a moth, but a butterfly. You'd think that might be cute. You'd be wrong.

He has great wings of black and orange, and dark skin marked with white dots across his face and torso. The white dots appear uncannily like eyes, so the overall impression is of being watched by a hundred dangerous things at once. No wonder birds avoid monarch butterflies. I want to scream and run, but I stand still and force a polite smile, as so many people meeting their significant others' families have done before.

"Are you all based on insects?" I ask Justice the question, but I don't bother to reply to the other mutant's question. He obviously didn't like me on sight, and the feeling is fairly mutual.

"Not all of us," Justice says. "Fury, this is Detective Holmes of the NYPD. She apprehended and subsequently dispatched Rage."

So much for not telling them I killed Rage.

"May he rest in peace," Fury says, giving me a look I do not appreciate. The hostility is palpable. I am not only unwelcome, I am grossly unpopular. I can feel the presence of others. They are not here in the room, but I sense them nearby. Listening. Learning.

I notice that Fury does not seem surprised to see me. Obviously, word was sent ahead of time, and not just about Rage. About me. This hive of mutant intelligence has been waiting for me. It has a plan for me. A plan I am not familiar with, and to which I have not been made privy.

Justice still has his grip on my hand. Using that hold, he leads me through the lobby. Fury takes up position on the other side of me. The energy shifts, and in an instant I am suddenly captive, a prisoner walking between two guards.

"Justice, you will regret this. If you are doing what I think you are doing, then you will find yourselves all in a..."

"Does she always talk this much?" Fury asks the question over my head.

"She's actually much less trouble when she's talking," Justice replies. "It's when she goes quiet that you really need to watch her."

Fuck it. Before they can get any deeper with me, I yank my hand from Justice, turn and book it toward the exit. I am smaller than them which makes me more nimble, and being more nimble gives me valuable seconds. They can't turn as fast as I can, but once they're on a straight path, they can beat their wings and easily overhaul me.

I am almost at the door when eight hands grip me. It's a lot of hands, and I am swung up and off the ground between the two mutant monsters. I can't even fight them, because all my limbs are controlled. They have me by my arms and legs, and there's no escape.

"Justice! Let me go!" I scream. "I do not consent to this. I have done enough. I want to go back to my old life."

"To the lonely apartment, and to the job that inexorably strips every vestige of innocence and joy from you? The one that turned you from someone who upheld the law into someone who took that law into her own hands and made her judge, jury, and executioner?"

"You said you were fine with that!?"

"I accept that what happened, happened. I understand my role in it. I failed you. And I failed Rage. I intend to stop failing."

They are carrying me away with long strides. I am being taken back into the bowels of this facility. The waiting room was not the only place where the 50's reigned supreme. Everything about these inner chambers is built in the style of the 40's and 50's. Smooth curves and wood panels, pastel colors and fascinating lines dominate what seems to be my new prison.

"Justice! They'll come for me! They'll find me, too. And then you know what will happen? They'll burn this fucking place to the ground. Let me go, you stupid sonofabitch!"

"Did you get a room ready for her as I asked?" He asks the question over my head.

"Yes," Fury says. "It's up here. We imagined you might have some trouble getting a human to agree to captivity."

Captivity. There's a fucking trigger word.

"Justice! What are you doing!?" I'm surprised, and I hate that I am surprised, because that means I wasn't paying attention. How did I not notice his intention to capture me?

"You need some time to think about things," he says. "This room is unoccupied."

They push open a door with a curve at the top. I don't know why that matters, but it does. There's a faint coziness about everything here being perpetually undermined by the oddness of it all.

I am thrust into the room. I turn around and give Justice my very best betrayed expression. I am fucking pissed, but I am also things beyond pissed, because this is so weird. Many weird things happen in the life of a New York detective, but this is beyond the weirdest. It's a little exciting. Shouldn't be, but is.

"I'll come and talk to you soon," he says.

"Maybe you will, maybe you won't. Turns out you're a huge fucking liar."

He gives me a stern look, because he has no shame, and shuts me in. I am left to explore my environment.

The room is bigger than my apartment. It is carpeted in baby blue, a hue which is carried up from the carpets to the matching drapes, walls, bedding, oh, and when I look up, ceiling. There are a few natural wood accents in the form of cabinets and the bed frame itself. Beige and blue appears to be my fate for now. An ensuite leading off the bedroom is similarly decorated, but it is pink, not blue. Pink tile, pink shower curtain, pink ceramic toilet and bath. It's a nightmare of cohesive design. The very notion of the color white appears to have been anathema to the person who outfitted these spaces.

It's not what I'd call good decor, but hey, someone thought it was good. They've given me what's very likely one of their best rooms.

"Oh my god, that's a television."

I suddenly realize that the big box at the end of the bed is not a piece of decorative whatever. It is a big box, very large, very rectangular, with an even bigger brown-gray screen and knobs. I should possibly be focusing on escape, but I wonder if this works. I turn a knob, hit a few buttons, and it makes a sound like a magnet turning on. The screen crackles, and a black and white image appears. It's an old tv show about cowboys. It's actually pretty interesting, or at least, it's enough to take my mind off this particular predicament until Justice returns.

I must have fallen asleep, because it is something o'clock when Justice wakes me up by sitting down on the bed beside me, one of his wings extending out to cover me.

"Are you feeling any better?" He asks the question almost kindly. I yawn. It is late. I am used to being a night owl, but I have been up all day as well as all night, and that is a bit much for anybody.

"What do you want, Justice? You've been lying to me since we began. You said you forgave me for killing Rage. But it was only because you knew you were going to bring me back here and imprison me in this time capsule for the rest of my life? No. Not going to happen. Your secrets were safe with me, but I am not safe with you."

"I am sorry you are angry with me, but keeping our secret is imperative. I could never allow you to continue on in the world, knowing what you know, seeing what you have seen. There is more at play here than you understand. You're in deeper than you know, metaphorically and literally."

My thoughts flick to Tessie. She has also seen and known. I hope she has the sense to stay well away from that spider, Order. He no doubt has plans to snatch her up and keep her quiet too.

"New York is safe from the moth predator that stalked the streets, and we are safe from the humans who might inadvertently tell our secrets," Justice says.

"If Order has fucking touched Tessie..."

"Don't worry about Tessie. Worry about yourself. Or rather, don't worry about yourself. There is a role here for you. A place. You can be of use here, and that is all you have ever wanted."

"What are you talking about?"

"I want you to stay here as a liaison between us and the world, not merely a prisoner, but an ally. We need humans we can trust, and there are precious few of those. You can go out, perform interactions in person, and..."

"Be an errand girl for mutant monsters."

"Sure, if you want to put it that way. But it would be better if you considered yourself a very privileged holder of a secret that has been kept for decades. You have no idea how you will be transformed here."

"Chief's expecting me back at work on Monday. There's no way I'm staying here to run errands, buddy. I came for the funeral."

"Since when does the killer attend the funeral?"

That question lands like a flying sidekick to the gut. It momentarily knocks the wind out of me.

"Surprisingly often, actually. But I can see your forgiveness isn't quite as forgiving as you pretended it was."

I am pissed. I do not like being lied to or lured. It's just ironic that Justice doesn't want to keep me captive here. He wants me to stay here as his ally and he's willing to imprison me until I Stockholm around to his way of thinking.

These mutants were not raised with any sort of generally accepted social values. He doesn't see anything wrong with what he is doing. This just makes sense to him. He's got me where he can control me and the rest, in theory at least, is time.

"I forgive you completely. But what I choose to do with you now is to change the life you were living, to keep you for myself, and to give you the chance to be part of something far more important than you can imagine. We are not random freaks. We are relics of an age of heroism. We are still able to do good, and you can help us."

"I already have people I help."

He sighs. "Will you not see sense?"

"Probably not. No. Not what you think is sense."

"Stubborn girl," he sighs. "That is part of why I love you."

"Love me?" I laugh. "You don't love me, Justice. You want to keep me. Love has the balls to let what it loves go. You're just another greedy fucker with an obsessive attachment."

Justice has the nerve to look hurt.

He's really not going to like what happens next.

I tried making a simple escape once. That didn't work. I can't just run away from Justice. I have to incapacitate him. Fortunately, I didn't just lie down in my prison bedroom and fall asleep without making preparations. I let him see me pick up the leg of a chair I removed earlier and hid under the baby blue bedspread.

"What do you think you're going to do with that?" He smirks at me, both pairs of arms folded over his chest as if I am the most pathetic, yet amusing thing he has ever seen.

I do not wield it against him. Instead, I hold it like a back-handed spear and drive it into the very center of the television as hard as I can. The screen shatters and there is a bright flash of fire and light of the kind that stun-locks his moth brain.

That's when I run, full speed, as hard and as fucking fast as I can. I have an unpleasant sensation of fullness in my midsection that prevents me from really getting up to speed, but I hope it's enough. I just have to get out of....

"No, you don't!"

Justice catches up with me just inside the lobby. I scream with outrage and despair as he grabs me up off my feet and begins chastising me immediately.

"That was a very bad idea," he growls. "Destruction of property, an assault on my senses. You should know better than to behave that way."

"Fuck off," I curse at him. I am not sorry, and I refuse to pretend to be.

"I wanted to put you in a comfortable room and make this easy for you, but you don't want comfort. You don't respond to reason. You want pain and you want anger. You crave intensity. And so you shall have it."

He yanks me up into his arms and carries me ever deeper. Behind all the cutesy 1950's decor lurks a horde of over-powered creatures who have no purpose but for the one given to them by their creator. They want to be heroes, but the world is past heroes now.

"Justice, you're acting crazy," I say. I know it's not going to help, but I feel justified saying it. "It's not appropriate, at all. In fact, this is illegal. And when you do illegal things, you end up in trouble."

I'm talking to him like he's a bad little boy. It amuses me to do so, because I know whatever comes next won't be good. Justice wants something from me. Actually, he wants every-thing from me.

~

The next room I find myself in maintains the curves and the sleek metalwork, but that is all. This is a cell, or a dungeon. It's empty aside from a few places where chains can hook into the walls. It's the sort of place made for keeping sentient things captive, a place for the breeding and breaking of monsters, and I suppose now, me.

"These cuffs are so cute," he says, plucking them out of my pocket. I never go out without a pair of them, and now they're being used on me, snapped around my wrists. He connects them to a chain, which is connected to the wall, all very businesslike and matter of fact. I notice he's blinking a lot. That little explosion might have actually done some damage. Couldn't have happened to a nicer abductor.

He begins to strip me. No more Mr Nice Mothman. He pulls my clothing off my body, cuts it where necessary. He makes me entirely naked, expecting it to have some effect on me, I imagine. He's forgotten that he fucked me the second time we met, and it never made me the slightest bit more submissive to him.

"I knew you would not agree to this. I knew you would need convincing," he mutters as he goes, almost talking to himself more than to me.

"See, a good guy, a hero, Justice, when he knows a woman won't agree to something, he doesn't go ahead and do it anyway. He respects her right to choose her own destiny. You're not a hero. You're just a creepy guy happy to keep a girl in the basement."

He chuckles, unashamed. "There is only one thing I could do right now that would disappoint you," he says. "And that would be let you go."

"Try it. See what happens."

"Not yet. You're not ready yet."

I sigh. "See. You're the same as..."

"I am not the same," he snaps. "You do not understand enough about the world, or the consequences of your actions. You think I can let you go, and you can return to your work an unchanged person. But you cannot."

"Why not."

"Because of what has taken place between your thighs. Because of the joining of our flesh, and the swelling of your interior."

"I don't know what the hell you're talking about."

"Of course not. I didn't just bring you into this chamber because it is more of a punishment. I brought you here because things are about to get messy."

"What do you mean, messy?"

He smiles again, and his tongue extends, unfurling down between my thighs, that precocious organ promising pleasure.

"Don't think you can distract me, Justice," I moan as he distracts me completely with those soft little licks and caresses that make my inner thighs tremble. No man gives oral pleasure this intense. It is good enough to make me find this captivity a little on the hot side. I cannot be held responsible for what happens now. He has taken me prisoner and that means I am at his mercy.

"Haven't you felt the slightest bit strange lately?" he asks between licks.

"I have felt nothing but strange lately," I reply. "You got a specific in that vague serving of bullshit?"

He chuckles in a *you'll see* sort of way that I particularly hate. This fucker knows something he is not telling me.

The more his unfurling tongue makes contact with the sensitive petals of my sex, probing for the nectar of my desire, the more those thoughts spur my arousal on. Perhaps there is some deep, secret part of me that enjoys this helplessness, this vulnerability. Maybe I can only indulge it in the most extreme of circumstances. I am discovering new facets to my nature even as I part my legs and arch my hips and give myself to my double-crossing lover.

The more he licks, the more I writhe, the more I feel pleasure snaking around my spine and up to my brain, then down to my toes. I am letting myself go. I am surrendering.

He has never been so generous with his oral pleasure before. Usually it is a precursor to sex, to his cock surging inside me. But he shows no interest in fucking me. He is feeding on me instead, drinking from my essence, and my body is responding as it has not done before.

Discharge is emerging from between my thighs. It's more than wetness from typical arousal, it's a thicker, more viscous liquid and there is a lot of it.

"Justice?"

He keeps licking me, one of his hands reaching up to stroke my hair soothingly. For a moment he lifts his tongue from my streaming sex so he can speak.

"It's alright," he says. "You are becoming what you were always destined to be. Relax and let it happen."

"Let what happen?"

There is a pressure, as though something is moving through from the inside of me, something that pushes out through my cervix and expands in my vaginal canal. It is like some strange reverse fucking, an intense and all too strange experience that feels much more than sexual.

"Justice!" I scream his name in real fear.

"Shhh... easy. It's okay. Just let it happen."

He grabs me by the hips between two pairs of his hands, keeping me still. I want to get up. I want to run. I need to flee, but I can't. I am a mess of arousal and terror. It is a potent combination.

"What is happening to me, Justice?"

"You're going to be a mother," he says, his eyes flashing at me. "You are giving birth."

As he speaks, something is crowning, sliding from my body. Something far bigger than has ever gone in. I know I am not pregnant, but something is happening. It doesn't hurt. It just feels like being stretched. It feels an odd kind of natural. A process is taking place inside me, something I cannot resist, cannot help, and cannot fight.

I look down between my thighs and see something large and creamy emerging from inside me. It is not a baby. It is something else. Something soft but tough, something that bears life. It emerges from me and rolls a few inches between my thighs, sitting pearlescent between myself and Justice.

"The fuck…"

No sooner do I vocalize my confusion than another one is coming, a second and then a third. Eggs emerge from my vagina, big, thick, globulous entities that pulse with life. The sensation is beyond strange. I am stretched beyond what I thought was possible. The first two are larger than the last, which seems to be a little bit of a biological afterthought.

Staring down at the ground between my mutant lover and I, I realize that I have laid three eggs. They are perfectly round, about the size of a cantelope. Their shells are thicker than I imagined, just beginning to harden as I touch them.

This is all so incredibly strange, I find myself not quite as disgusted and horrified as I might otherwise be, simply because I can't be sure it is all real. I feel stretched and I ache, but there is a certain hormonal surge, a happiness in the depths of my gut. I feel proud of these three round spheres, these very large jewels of life. I don't feel motherly, but I do feel somehow invested. It's chemical, that's all, just the reaction of a being when other beings emerge from it. Programmed in by nature so we don't eat our young.

"In nine months, these will hatch, and new life will emerge from them. You have become the mother of a new generation of heroes," Justice explains.

"Do I need to sit on them?"

"You're not a chicken," he chuckles. "They will stay here. They will grow. First they will emerge as pupae. They will feed. And then, when they have fed enough, they will turn into chrysalis and they will emerge as their adult forms, though still young."

"How long do they feed?"

"Four or five years. Then the chrysalis stage takes twelve to thirteen years. When they emerge, they will be fully grown adults. Eighteen years old or so."

"Oh, so I'm not going to parent these guys so much as my kids are going to wriggle around here until they spin themselves into sacks and then emerge not knowing me at all?"

"They'll have genetic memories of you, and there will be no doubt that they are of you. I hope they have your beautiful coloring, your bravery, your self-possession. Your ability to act in the face of danger, and to adapt to strange circumstances and times. You are quite a specimen, Sally."

"Ugh. Not my name. Call me anything besides that name."

"What if I were to call you my wife?"

There is a sweetness to the request that my New York attitude compels me to reject.

"Are you serious? You abducted me and implanted your seed in me. You had me bear your young, and even now, I am chained in the basement of your lair. These are not the circumstances of a wedding proposal."

"Fair enough," he laughs. "You're right. Besides. What difference does it make, really. You are mine, ring or not, ceremony or not. You are the mother of my young."

Fuck me. That is true. I am the mother of his young. He has hijacked my genetic material and used my womb and he has reproduced with me none the wiser until it was far too late. I have been violated.

"How did this happen so quickly? Does it happen every time we, you know..."

"You must have been ovulating when we first mated. My seed finds the human female egg, changes the way the cell divides, and in most cases, causes a duplication or triplication. You were very receptive to my seed. You are a natural mate for me. We will breed hundreds, perhaps thousands of heroes." His red eyes gleam with excitement. "You and I will make this broken world whole again."

"I am not going to pump out mutant babies for you, Justice."

"Are you sure about that, mother of heroes?" He smiles at me. "You birthed them so easily and so naturally. You have provided the vault with the first new eggs in many years. The future lies between your thighs."

This is flattering, and strange, and terrifying, and disgusting, and sweet, and wrong. It is so many things. None of them make sense or are easy to come to terms with. I thought I was the captive of a mutant monster, but I am more than that. I seem to be the first person to ever create a sexual alliance with one of these creatures. Justice loves me in his very own twisted way. He has chosen to procreate with me. He has made me his mate.

"You will see soon enough," he says. "This is the future you have chosen, whether you understand it or not, whether you know it or not, this is the path of your happiness. Together, you and I will build a life and a family. Now. Rest. You will need it. Laying eggs takes great energy."

Maybe that is why I am not freaking out. Maybe I am just too tired. Maybe I don't have the energy to fight this oddness. Maybe it feels intimate, sweet, and perhaps even loving.

Maybe it does. For an hour. But not two. I wake with the knowledge that it is daylight outside. I am naked and I am aching. I no longer feel whatever hormonal influence made me so calm during the laying of the eggs. Justice has moved away from me in our sleep, and he has wrapped himself around them.

Justice is cute when he is dormant. He almost looks human, but for those large wings of his, now spread out in a protective span over his clutch. I made him a father last night, but he did not make me anything more than a prisoner. No matter how sweet he is in his sleeping state, I cannot pretend I matter. We have known one another for a matter of days, and in that time he has used me as a thing, treated me as a pawn, and finally turned me into his captive.

He made a mistake when he used my own cuffs on me. I know how to get out of my own cuffs. I don't even need a tool. I can snap out of them with a series of quick motions, and I do.

I pull my clothes back on and make my way out of the facility. There's nobody to stop me. I walk up and out of the vault without a moment's hesitation. I refuse to feel guilty for this decision and these actions. Justice will be hurt, but he never cared about my feelings, and therefore I cannot afford to care about his.

The truck has been unloaded, but it remains where it was. I don't know what they did with what is left of Rage, and I do not care. I want out of here. I want to put this entire creepy fucking interlude behind me.

I am up and behind the wheel when a creature of flashing orange and black lands in front of the truck. It is Fury. The Monarch. And he is terrifying in the light of day. Fortunately, I am not alone. I have a several ton truck at my disposal, and I am not afraid to use it.

"Get out of the way," I shout out the window. "I thought you fuckers slept all day."

"You forget, I am a creature of the day," he laughs. "You will not leave this place so easily."

I put the truck in gear. "I am going to turn you into a smear on the windshield if you don't get the absolute fuck out of my way."

He cocks his head at me, and gives me a little mocking smile "How many of us are you going to kill, human?"

"It depends how many of you try to keep me from going home."

"Justice begged us to allow you to come to this facility, sent message after message, and here you are, so ungrateful, desperate to leave."

"Did he demand you allow me as a human to infiltrate your little lair? Did he tell you I killed Rage, but it didn't matter because he'd already knocked me up? And did you let him bring me even though you didn't want him to because you wanted those eggs too? Well, you got your fucking eggs. Now. Get out of my way."

Fury laughs. "You are so badly disciplined. I know he has had little time with you, but surely he could have taught you some manners. You may be his, but in our world, you belong to all of us in some way."

"Well, in my world, you're all one large can of fly spray away from being irrelevant. Get the fuck out of my way and hope I don't come back with a bug bomb."

"And destroy your precious little ones?"

He's talking about the eggs. I don't want to think about them. They are a certain kind of strangeness I can't wrap my mind around. I don't feel about them the way I would feel about a baby, but then again I don't have to feed them several times a night or teach them how to not shit themselves constantly. Eggs are easier, but they're way less cute.

"Humans don't get attached to eggs," I tell him. "They're nothing to me."

"It is common for a young female to reject her first clutch," he says. "But I'm telling you, if I let you drive out of here, you'll be back, except instead of coming back to your mate and clutch, you'll be coming back to trouble."

"Oh, is that right?"

"It is," he says, folding his arms over his chest. He's a scary looking motherfucker. Taking advice from him is not easy but murdering him by running him over isn't exactly in the cards either.

"Can you get the fuck out of my way?"

"Can you get out of the truck like a good little girl?"

I curse under my breath. This is getting fucking crazy. I rev the engine and blow the horn, which makes a hell of a noise, sending birds flying into the air for miles around.

Fury doesn't move. He stands there, unimpressed.

"If you were mine, I'd wash your mouth out with soap and whip your hide until you begged for mercy. And you wouldn't be getting such frequent breedings, either. I'd make sure you understood cock was a privilege."

"If you were mine, I'd put you in a jar," I snap back.

"Oh, yes, the insect jokes, very droll. Why don't you come out here and tell one? See what I do to you, as you have abandoned your mate and clutch."

"Fuck off."

"You don't want Justice, I'll take you."

"No, you fucking won't."

"Someone will. Something will. Or it won't. Is that what you want? A life without your mate and clutch?"

"Dude! I was single last fucking week. It takes longer than that to bond with someone and want to raise human caterpillars with them. Are they are going to be caterpillars with baby faces Christ! Or something worse?! I do not need that in my life. I need to escape this freak show, before..."

"See. I knew it. Afraid of your clutch," Fury says. "Very common. Modern women want live young. They're obsessed with having living, squirming, crying, small humans emerge from their bodies in a painful orgy of blood and sometimes death."

"What do you mean, modern women?" This conversation is absolutely insane, and that is saying a lot given all the conversations I have had in my lifetime. I can only imagine what Randy Carrot would make of this. "People have babies. It's what they do."

"It's not what you did."

"I'm not. This isn't... Stand aside and let me go."

"I told Justice I would keep watch while he slept, and I intend to do that. I do not think you are the murderer you appeared to be when you came here. I think you are a confused young woman with a destiny she wants to fight, because everybody always fights their destiny."

"They do, huh."

"Sure. Whatever the obvious course of action is, people don't want it. They want to be something either more or less than what they are instead of just following the path destiny has laid out for them. You were made to be Justice's mate. You have already helped him and us. You have shown courage and honor, and..."

"And been trapped in an egg-laying facility for my troubles."

"Would you rather he'd left you alone to have those eggs at home, perhaps in the bath? Or perhaps in your workplace? Would you like to have become the focus of a new series, *Help, I Didn't Know I Was Laying?*"

"You watch too much tv," I snort. "He could have told me. He tricked me. I thought I was coming here for a funeral, not to become his brood queen."

"Really? You didn't put two and two together when he wanted you to meet his family?"

"No! No, I didn't! And even if you do try to normalize this, meeting a guy's family does not usually mean being trapped in his basement and producing them out of your own vagina."

"Justice may not have handled this perfectly, but he was raised here in isolation, as were we all. Our interactions with humanity were limited. He is not trying to hurt you. Nor am I."

"Good. Then get out of the way."

Fury shrugs and steps aside.

Finally. I put my foot on the gas and... nothing. I don't press it down. I don't know why. I just sit there, idling, wondering why I feel so strange and conflicted. Now that I'm no longer actively being kept captive, the idea of rushing back to New York isn't as appealing as I insisted it was.

I do know what my life is like there. It is quite sad, in many ways. I have no attachment to anybody besides Tessie. I am a tool for the chief to use, and I took a lot of pride in that for a long time, but am I going to feel the same way knowing I've left the greatest mystery of all behind? And my eggs. Are my eggs okay? I suddenly feel a welling of concern for those little white globules.

"Fuck," I curse, slamming the steering wheel with my hand.

The cab door opens. Fury offers me his hand.

Silently, I turn off the engine, and let him help me out.

I wait for his smug words, his judgement, maybe even some kind of pain.

Fury looks down at me from his great height, his dark eyes absolutely eerie with their two round whites dead in the center. I brace myself for what is about to emerge from his mouth.

"How about some breakfast?"

11

"You can't keep me captive. You can't make me do anything."

"Yes," Justice says. "I am beginning to understand that."

I have spent the day at the vault, waiting for him to wake up so I can give him a piece of my mind. A lot of what he did here was absolutely uncool, and we need to get that fucking straight.

We are talking in the blue room I was first put into. The television has been removed and the floor cleaned. Fury told me I deserved a good spanking for breaking it. I told him he needed to find someone else to punish. He said that might not be such a bad idea.

"Do you really want to take yourself back to a world you were always trying to escape? Those books, you had thousands of them, all little portals to other worlds. A home like yours is nothing more than the manifestation of the need to get away," Justice says.

"You don't understand what a book is," I tell him. "It's an escape, but it doesn't mean I don't want to live my life. It means I want a bigger life, a broader life, one seen through the eyes of others. It does not mean I want to be kept in a dungeon getting pumped full of semen. Being used as a brooder for mutant eggs was definitely not on the agenda. You're not offering me freedom. You're offering me captivity."

"I am not a true monster," he says with a sigh. "I will not keep you here against your will. I chained you for your first laying because I did not want you to panic and thrash and destroy the eggs before they had a chance to toughen their shells. But if you wish to leave here, I will not stop you."

He's missing the point. He always misses the point. I can see that I am going to spend the rest of my life explaining these things to him.

"You have to let me choose you," I tell him. "You can't make decisions for me. You have to tell me the truth and let me make my own decisions. It's the only way you'll ever know if I really love you or not."

Justice braces himself. "I know you cannot love a creature like me."

Aw, Christ. Now it hits me. He thinks he has to keep me locked up because a basic bitch human with just four limbs like me couldn't possibly ever love a mutant. He has no idea that women always love monsters, one way or another.

"Your wings and eyes are the least of your flaws. Knocking me up and chaining me, that's what you have to work on. You've never asked me if I wanted to be fucked. Not once."

"That first time... I felt you wanted it. I felt the way your body writhed, I smelled the scents it produced when I pinned you in place, I experienced the exquisite grip of your body, and I saw the way you looked at me. I may have misunderstood all these things. I may have wanted you more than you wanted to be wanted."

"You know what the worst part of this is? I wanted you too, but then you acted like such a complete fucking jerkwad at absolutely every turn."

He wraps his arms around me and pulls me close. His embrace is surprisingly gentle. He is taking care of me, reaching the parts of me that want him without even trying.

"Let me be your big, bad, dominant jerk," he purrs, seducing me with his tone. "Let me be the worst decision you ever made. Let us be."

Fuck. I want this. I want him. I don't want to be so consumed with wanting. I want to be disgusted and offended. I want to be normal. Why can I never be normal?

"Stop fighting yourself," he urges me. "I can sense what you want. I can feel it in you. Can you not feel it too?"

"Of course I can feel it, asshole. But it's like I said. You don't need to take me prisoner. You have to let me choose you every day. That's how love works. It's choosing and being chosen again and again and again."

"You're right," he agrees. "And now I choose to be inside you."

He kisses me, and I melt. I want to be with him. I want to live his monstrous life. I want to discover what the hell a mutant caterpillar baby with my eyes looks like. I want to love him, and I want to be loved by him.

My thighs part for him, as they have from our first aerial embrace. He was right. My body has always responded to him this way, with passion and desire. He may have been engineered by scientists, but nature made me for him.

"Come with me," he says, taking me by the hand and leading me outside. The night is cool and calm. The full moon hangs heavy in the sky. Justice wraps his arms around me and lifts me up in his arms, powerful wings spreading and beating as we rise into the air.

"I'm going to fill you up," he promises as the night wind makes our hair flow together, mine red, his black. That filthy promise is accompanied by the midair disrobing of my lower body.

He pulls my pants and underwear down, his cock finding the stretched chalice between my thighs. I have been well used, and that means his massive manhood can slide right up inside me with one harsh and possessive thrust. Impaled on my lover, I lift my eyes to the moon, and I surrender to his lust.

"I am going to breed you full of eggs, and I'm going to pleasure you as you lay them. You're going to take my cock and bear my young as many times as I can make you."

I come on his cock fucking hard just at those words. My pussy grips his thick monster rod and does her best to milk him of his seed, but he's not ready to give it to me yet. I have to withstand a lot more of his filthy talk and his rough ravaging before I am rewarded with his potent cum.

"Good girl," he praises, rocking me back and forth on his rod. "That's such a good fucking girl. Come for me again. Show me how much you want my seed."

I look down beneath our bodies. The ground rushes below, the sky beside, but all I can see is the lewd stretching of my lips, his cock buried deep inside me. We are joined, he and I, two very different monsters locked together in the act of breeding.

I've fought my urges, and I've fought him. I've tried to resist this inevitability because it does not match what I thought I wanted for myself. But this chemistry, this embrace, this belonging and possession. This is irresistible.

I stretch out and I take him deep inside me, I give myself to him, and to the vault and to the clutch. There is no choice. There is no option. It has to be him. Forever.